Books
by Len Giovannitti

The Prisoners of Combine D

The Decision to Drop the Bomb
  (co-author)

The Man Who Won the Medal of Honor

The Man
Who Won
the Medal
of Honor

The Man
Who Won
the Medal
of Honor

Len
Giovannitti

RANDOM HOUSE
NEW YORK

All rights reserved under International
and Pan-American Copyright Conventions.
Published in the United States
by Random House, Inc., New York,
and simultaneously in Canada
by Random House of Canada Limited, Toronto.

Library of Congress Cataloging in Publication Data
Giovannitti, Len, 1920–
The man who won the Medal of Honor.
I. Title.
PZ4.G512Man   PS3557.I57   813'.5'4   73-5003
ISBN 0-394-48776-1

Manufactured in the United States of America

9   8   7   6   5   4   3   2

First Edition

For the poet who wrote:

All that you worship, fear and trust
I kick into the sewer's maw
And fling my shaft and my disgust
Against your gospel and your law.

ARTURO GIOVANNITTI

And for his grandson, David, age 19

And for those who kept the faith

The Man
Who Won
the Medal
of Honor

1.

My lawyers—there are two—are preparing my defense on the grounds of insanity at the time I committed the act for which I am now awaiting trial. I have refused stubbornly to go along with them. They passionately insist that it is the only grounds on which they can hope to save my life. With greater passion I insist that such a defense is a denial of the principles by which I have lived. I cannot deny those principles. Of course, my lawyers know far less about my principles and me than I do. And I cannot tell them more because I do not believe they would understand. And if they did it would not help them in their work. Quite the contrary, I think it would hamper their efforts in my defense. So we are at odds.

When I first got the idea to write down the essentials of my experience for you—my peers (as my lawyers are not because they have a vested interest in me)—I asked the jailer for a dictionary. I wanted to look up the definitions of two words that concern me greatly. He provided me with the only dictionary available in the prison: *Webster's New World Dictionary*. It sufficed. These are the words and their definitions:

3

Insanity: specifically, *in law,* any form or degree of mental derangement or unsoundness, permanent or temporary, that makes a person incapable of what is regarded *legally* as normal, rational conduct or judgment.

Rational: having the ability to reason logically, as by drawing conclusions from inferences; often connotes the absence of emotionalism.

I believe I am rational and therefore not insane. I acted rationally, not insanely. You be my judge. This is my story.

○

Let me put last things first. I am a Medal of Honor recipient. I received the news of this honor on a pleasant day in July. The telegram arrived in a letter. It was from the Secretary of Defense. It read in part: AS SECRETARY OF DEFENSE IT IS MY PLEASURE TO INFORM YOU THAT YOU HAVE BEEN AWARDED THE MEDAL OF HONOR FOR HEROISM IN BATTLE ABOVE AND BEYOND THE CALL. . . . It went on to detail the conditions under which I had acted to save the American lives of my patrol in Vietnam by destroying an enemy machine-gun emplacement and killing four of the enemy without regard for my own safety. It concluded with the request that I and my family attend ceremonies at the White House at 10 A.M. on August 28, at which time I would be decorated personally by the President.

The absurdity of the news evoked peals of laughter from me. Someone of some authority had made a mistake that had snowballed through the chains of command clear up to the White House. It was a ludicrous error and yet, as I held that telegram in my hand, I felt it was a fitting climax to my year of combat in Vietnam. Now, of course, I feel differently because my life is at stake.

I had laughed at the news because I had never—in that long year of patrols and gunship missions—killed a single enemy soldier or civilian. I had been very careful not to. On the other hand, I had killed a number of American soldiers—precisely, a private, three corporals, a lieutenant, a colonel and a one-star general. Until now, no one knew I

4

was responsible for their deaths. Until now, I could tell no one. But now I no longer need to keep silent.

○

Sitting in my prison cell these past months I've had nothing but time to think back on that year in Vietnam. Nothing to distract me from reconstructing in minute detail the circumstances and events of that soldiering year. When it was over and I returned to the States, I had some difficulty putting my experiences out of my mind. But I had done what I had to do without a flicker of doubt, without later remorse. It never occurred to me that I would find it necessary to recall those events and painstakingly record them here. I believe I could have lived and died untroubled by them. No one would ever have known what I had done. But the unexpected telegram changed all that.

2.

And now to put first things first. I am twenty years old. I was orphaned at the age of eleven. I still think of myself as an orphan because I am alone in the world to this day and more alone today than I have ever been since the day I was orphaned.

That day I was in an airplane with my parents flying to a vacation in California when the plane struck a mountain peak in the Rockies and exploded. I was hurtled through the air and landed, without injury, in a snowbank. The details of the crash I have long forgotten. The events thereafter I remember well. I'll tell them briefly.

When the rescuers took me to the hospital in Denver and I was found fit, I was told my parents had died in the crash. I was then asked about other relatives and I said I had no relatives. They persisted with their questions. There must be an aunt, an uncle, a cousin? I told them my parents' families had been killed by Hitler in the war. My parents had been the only survivors. They had met in a concentration camp and afterwards had married and come to America where I was born. I told them all that as I had been told by my father. But there must be friends back in New York? I

6

thought of one or two. I didn't like them. I said there were no friends. They made an effort to find someone in New York who would be responsible for me. They found no one.

On the third day, I was released from the hospital and placed in an orphanage in Denver. At first I cried a lot because I missed my parents. But I got used to my new life. The orphanage wasn't bad. The staff people were kind to me, and in my first year there I was recommended for adoption several times but nothing came of it. Everyone soon realized that no one wanted to adopt an eleven-year-old. It was just as well. I didn't want new parents. I only wanted to grow up quickly and be on my own. I stayed at the orphanage for seven years but I never felt it was my home. It was an institution and I left it, on my eighteenth birthday, for another institution—the United States Army.

3.

I enlisted in the army because it offered me an immediate escape from the orphanage, where my time was up, and because it provided a haven of sorts and three squares a day plus a pay check. I discovered, before I was eighteen, that while I wanted to be on my own I was not yet ready for it. I needed a transition from the protection of the orphanage to the competition of the world outside. The army offered the only transition I could think of. At eighteen the orphanage turned me out and the army welcomed me in.

At the time I didn't think of the army as an institution engaged in a war in Vietnam. That may seem strange to you considering that we had been fighting there for many years, but the orphanage had walled me in from a society at war. It was a world of its own with a separate life. Oh, I knew vaguely about the race riots, the campus unrest and Vietnam. It was all there to be seen on the television news, but I paid it little attention and gave it no thought. Newspapers, too, were available, but you'd be surprised how easy it is for a teenage boy to avoid reading them. Television and the movies, of course, I did not ignore for they provided me with an escape from the routine of the orphanage. The film army I knew was made up of cavalry units that killed the Indians and of infantry and tanks and bombers that blasted the Germans. It was a romantic army of comradeship and heroism. The army I entered in the spring of '68 was something else.

○

In basic training there was little comradeship and no heroism, not then and not later as it turned out. But there was an enemy and he had a name—several names, I should say. Depending on your drill instructor, he was called "the VC" or "Charlie" or "gink" or "gook" or "slopehead." And he was to be feared and respected because he was good at his trade and because he was fighting on home ground and mostly because he gambled his life for yours "no matter what the fucking odds are against him."

"And one more thing," every drill sergeant drilled into us. "Charlie isn't a man like you are. Physically, I mean. He's small and skinny. He's a ten-year-old kid or a seventy-year-old man without a tooth in his head but quick enough to put a knife in your belly or your back. And he's the girl you're thinking of fucking on your chow break. And he might be a slanty-eyed old lady cooking in her straw hootch. Yeah, yeah. You think I'm pulling your dick but you just better listen and listen hard. One time this old gook woman threw a bowl of scalding hot gook food in the face of my buddy. Then she was on him with a knife longer than your mother's tongue. She didn't give a damn that I was there. She'da killed the blinded bastard if I hadn't stuck her with my bayonet clean through her gullet. Yeah, yeah. That's what your bayonets is for. Close quarters. And when your clip is empty. Yeah, empty 'cause you used it up pacifying them slopeheads. But the point of my story is not the use of the bayonet. It's recognizing the enemy. Know who he is? He's every motherfucker in Veetnam that ain't white."

"But sergeant, I ain't . . ."

"Or black," the sergeant added and he grinned. "Any red-faced Indians in the company?"

9

"Ah'm a red-*neck*, sergeant," a voice drawled. "Don't y'all slit my gullet."

"Don't wear no black pajamas," the sergeant said, "and you'll be okay in Veetnam. Now let's get on with the bayonet drill. You got a lot of killing to learn."

○

By the end of my basic training I hated the army. It was an institution in a constant state of tension because of two opposing factions: the one, a hard-core group of professionals that maintained the machinery of authority; the other, raw recruits—most of them draftees—who resented that authority and schemed to disrupt the machinery. I belonged to a third group of enlisted men who accepted authority chiefly to keep out of trouble. It was not easy. Living with the discontented, we were often punished for their violations of the rules. We had little recourse and it rankled. Yet I was able to cope with the situation better than most. My seven years of organized routine in a benevolent orphanage had prepared me for the stricter discipline of the army. I didn't question authority. I kept to myself and I got by.

But when we got our orders to ship out, I felt unprepared to face the enemy. The drill instructors' efforts to develop the killer instinct in me had failed. Each time I was commanded to plunge my bayonet into the stuffed dummy and shout "Kill!" I tensed up and bungled the thrust. I was no more proficient at the other skills of hand-to-hand combat. I found karate and judo as repugnant as bayonet drill. My instructors were disgusted with me. I couldn't blame them. I had no stomach for the job they were preparing me for and no amount of warning had any effect. If, as they told me, my life depended on slashing a man's throat or gouging out his eyes, then my chances for survival were slim.

To my surprise and satisfaction, I did redeem myself on the gunnery range. I quickly mastered the simple art of squeezing the trigger, not pulling it, and earned an expert marksmanship rating with the rifle.

Fortunately, as it turned out, I never had to encounter the enemy in hand-to-hand fighting, but my marksmanship with a rifle served me well.

4.

In Vietnam it doesn't take very long for an infantryman to become a combat veteran. At the end of two weeks, I had witnessed brutality and violent death. And I was learning rapidly to take care of myself.

My platoon was camped on a plateau in the Central Highlands outside a hamlet called Cam Binh. The mountain people gave us no trouble. But the valley and the hills to the west were VC territory. Our job was to conduct search-and-destroy patrols in the valley: in essence, to find and kill the enemy using whatever firepower was available—preferably choppers and ground artillery. One quickly learned to avoid taking on the VC with only mortars and rifles. If you were close enough to kill them with hand-held weapons you were close enough to get killed. By the summer of '68 no one was taking that risk unnecessarily. On the other hand, the VC, without choppers and with limited artillery, were highly motivated to get within rifle range of us. The difference in our attitudes made it clear to me, early on, that they were fighting to win while we were fighting to stay alive for our 365 days. My drill instructor was right. The VC risked their lives, no matter the odds, to kill us. The same was not true for us. If the odds were not heavily with us we avoided a direct encounter. It was a policy of attrition that was wearing us down faster than it was them.

○

My first experience with death came on the third day of my arrival at camp. Patrols into the valley were rotated through the four squads that made up the company. That third day it was my squad's turn. None of us replacements had been picked for the patrol. The night before, in selecting the four men he would lead, the sergeant had told all of us the VC were reported to be filtering down from the hills into the valley. Platoon headquarters wanted to know why.

Looking over the faces of the new recruits, the sergeant said it was a job for veterans. He made it clear that if the VC were building up in the valley he didn't want any "frightened fuckups" backing him up. That didn't mean the new men would be coddled. He guaranteed that we'd all get our bellyful of gooks quick enough.

I didn't mind being called a frightened fuckup. It seemed to me a fair appraisal coming from a man doing his second tour in Vietnam. He had a better idea of what to expect from untested replacements than I did. I was relieved to be excused from the detailed briefing of the patrol.

That night I went to bed with the comforting thought that I was safe for the time being. It didn't last very long. It seemed as if I'd hardly fallen asleep when I was roughly awakened by someone punching my shoulder. As I bolted up in bed, the blanket was pulled from my body. A flashlight illuminated the blackness of the tent. For a moment I panicked, thinking it was the VC, but the voice of my attacker was reassuring. "Your name David Glass?"

"Yeah. Who the hell are you?" My hands trembled.

"Sergeant Stone. Who the hell did you think it was?"

"I don't know. The VC."

He snorted. "Charlie doesn't wake you up. He puts you

13

to sleep. Get dressed on the double. And don't forget your helmet and rifle. You're going on patrol in half an hour."

I blinked and shook my head to clear the sleep. "How come? I thought you didn't want any fuckups."

"Don't smart-ass me, soldier. You're a goddamn replacement and this morning I need a replacement. Corporal Hudson got sick. You're elected backup man."

"Why me?"

"Why not? Now get your ass out of that sack and get hustling. You got five minutes to get down to the mess tent for a hearty breakfast and a light briefing." He was out of the tent before I was out of the bed.

"What about supplies, rations?" I called after him.

"At the mess," he shouted back. "Five minutes."

In the darkness, I cursed for two minutes and dressed in three. My tentmate snored away. Why couldn't it have been him? Why not?

I shivered on the way to the mess. The days were hot and dry on the plateau but the nights were cold—good for sleeping but lousy for patrols. Nothing was good for patrols.

The sergeant and the other three were putting away eggs and coffee when I entered the mess. No one looked up. I got my soggy eggs and hot coffee and slid onto the bench across from the sergeant.

"This is our replacement—Glass," the sergeant said. "That's his name, like in broken."

The others grinned and went on eating. The sergeant rattled off their names and they nodded in turn. The names bounced right off me. I didn't find out who was who until we were two hours out on patrol and I needed them. Sergeant Stone was something else. I never forgot him or his name for the next 362 days.

I tried eating my eggs but I had no appetite and pushed them aside. "You better eat up," the sergeant said. "You won't get any hot food for the next two days."

"Two days?"

"Two days if you're lucky."

"I thought the patrol came back at night."

14

The sergeant gave me a benevolent smile. "Now where did you hear that, son?"

I measured the sergeant for a moment. I decided he was big and burly enough and old enough and experienced enough to call me son if he wanted to. I figured I was going to need him more than he needed me.

"I heard it around."

"Well, son," he went on in his condescending tone. "Some patrols stay out for a day, some for two days or five." He paused to catch the attention of the others. "And some patrols stay out there forever."

I guess my face recorded the alarm the sergeant expected because one of the others said, "Lay off, sarge. Stop scaring the kid."

I smiled weakly at him. He was blond and baby-faced. He looked my age except for his pale blue eyes. They were old.

The big, black guy sitting next to me said, "You going to eat your eggs, Glass?"

I shook my head and pushed the plate to him. He grunted his thanks and spooned them up.

"Okay, finish up and load your gear while I brief Glass here."

The sergeant's face was serious now and his voice flat, all business, as he laid out the whole plan: He was the patrol leader with Corporal Thomas second-in-command. The patrol was going down into the valley and across the river to reconnoiter around the ravine at the base of the western hills.

The sergeant unfolded a map on the table and indicated the area with his finger. Intelligence had reports that the VC were stockpiling equipment in the ravine, probably in caves. The mission's main objective was to collect any information to confirm or correct that intelligence. Any additional data collected—VC trails, campsites, minefields— would be greatly appreciated, the sergeant said, allowing himself a small smile that quickly dissipated.

It would take a half-day to get to the ravine and a half-day to get back, leaving twenty-four hours to reconnoiter the objective. The patrol would stay together at all times. No one was to wander off to investigate anything on his own. We would move in a cluster where we had the protection of the foliage but out in the open, across fields and fording the river, we would march single file at five-yard intervals. If we ran across any VC no one was to fire unless fired upon. The primary purpose of the patrol was to avoid direct combat and get back in one piece with its information. The sergeant glowered at me to be sure I understood and I nodded thoughtfully.

"One more thing," he said. "Every Vietnamese in that valley is an enemy. You understand that? I don't care if it's a toothless old man sitting under a tree or a kid pissing in the river. Stay clear. I'll handle that situation."

Again I nodded, thinking of my drill instructor's advice in basic. I pictured the enemy as an army of toothless old men and little boys backed up by old women brandishing bread knives.

"Any questions?"

I had a hundred but I knew they'd get answered soon enough so I asked just one. "Which guy is Corporal Thomas?"

Sergeant Stone heaved a sigh of disgust. "The black. He's a good soldier. You do just what he says."

I met the sergeant's steely gaze. "Why not?"

He got the point but retorted indirectly: "Okay, Glass. You better piss out that coffee or it'll be running down your legs in a couple of hours." He pointed to the others at the end of the mess tent. "Then pick up your gear. It's all laid out for you."

Some of my questions were answered when I loaded my gear—grenades, flares, ammunition, medical supplies. I felt considerably relieved when I noticed Corporal Thomas packing a field radio. We wouldn't be out there completely on our own. But why the fuck hadn't the sergeant told me we'd be in radio communication? And with whom? Platoon headquarters? Artillery? Choppers? All three? I had no basis for knowing that my briefing had been very brief. Regular briefings were spelled out and support was standard operating procedure. But I'd been drafted under emergency conditions, unfortunately without any previous experience. Stone's disgust with my one question was probably disappointment in me for not asking the other ninety-nine. I realized he would have reassured me but I didn't want him to think I was a frightened fuckup before we even started out. It was a stupid failure of communication no radio could help. I wasn't going to let it happen again.

○

It was five in the morning and still dark when we left the camp and started down the western slope of the plateau into the valley. With Sergeant Stone and Corporal Thomas leading the way, we followed a winding trail. It was fairly steep and the weight of my backpack climbed up on my shoulders, thrusting my head forward, making me top-heavy and threatening to tumble me heels over head. My pack was slung too high but there was no stopping to adjust it. Moreover, the pack straps were loose and with each bobble of the pack the straps pulled into my shoulders.

The forced marches in basic were poor preparation for the real thing. First, the terrain had been mostly flat. Second, every man was raw, just like you, and you could bitch freely to relieve yourself as you marched. Third, no place in America could duplicate the wet heat that rose up from that Vietnam valley. It was like walking into a cauldron of steam. A half-hour on the trail and I couldn't believe I had been sleeping under a blanket only an hour before. But mostly, on those marches in basic, I didn't have to worry about toothless old men lying in wait to slit my throat or shatter my sweating, pulsing head with a bullet. No sir. After half an hour down that trail I was ready to call it quits. I was too young to suffer so much so soon. My adjustment to the situation was to pray that *old* Sergeant Stone was feeling the same need for a rest that

I was. No such luck. He plodded ahead, holding a steady pace. Corporal Thomas, with a pack bigger than mine and the weight of the field radio to boot, stayed right up the sergeant's· ass. The other two—a tall, skinny, freckle-faced redhead, who could have doubled for a Raggedy Andy doll, and the blond kid with the old eyes—lagged easily behind, whispering from time to time and glancing back sympathetically at my plight.

We had the protection of the darkness as well as the foliage, but the narrowness of the trail didn't permit us to bunch up in a cluster and I was feeling alone, struggling to keep the pace. I began to worry about falling too far back and getting killed quietly by an Indian brave as the heroic column moved forward to meet the enemy. My fantasy gave impetus to my weary legs and I mustered the extra strength to catch up. As if aware of my fears, the blond kid fell back beside me.

"Hold on, Glass," he muttered. "Lean back as you go down. Don't hunch forward. Let the pack hold you back. Take the weight on the base of your spine, not your shoulders. Your straps are too loose."

"Yeah. I know now."

"Stay with it. The sergeant will call a break and I'll tighten your pack. He's putting out strong because of you. He's got sixteen months in this asshole war and he's still proving himself to scared punks. But he's getting ready for a halt. I can feel it in my legs. I've been out with him before. If that black sonofabitch stops climbing up his asshole we'll have time for a joint. I could use one. Hold on kid. I'll fix you up proper."

"Thanks, uh—"

"Cooper. Private Richard Cooper. I'm called Blondy. Three hundred and thirty-three days in this asshole and thirty-two left to go. Stay close, Glass. I'm going to make it."

"What happens to me after thirty-two days?"

"You find yourself another lucky asshole." He laughed. I couldn't muster a grin.

18

Up ahead, the sergeant called out, "We'll rest for five minutes. Smoke up."

The trail widened and leveled out in a small clearing. Sergeant Stone and the redhead were sitting on the ground, leaning against their packs. Corporal Thomas was still standing, looking down the trail ahead. The first light of dawn filtered through the trees. I dropped at my feet and Blondy squatted beside me. Empty cartons of C-rations were strewn about, left by patrols that had passed through.

Blondy adjusted my pack, lowering it into the small of my back, and then tightened the straps crisscrossing my chest. I felt much better and started to light a cigarette when Blondy stopped me. "Wait a second and you can try one of mine." His pale eyes brightened.

He placed a tissue of cigarette paper on the ground and filled it carefully with some dark, stringy tobacco. Then he rolled the paper around it, twisted the ends closed and lifted it delicately to his lips. A quick flip of his tongue along the open edge and he sealed the roll. He lit up and inhaled slow and long, his eyes closed. Smiling, he passed it to me. "Take a deep drag and hold it down as long as you can."

I held it and looked at the sergeant, a few feet away. His back was to me.

"Quick," Blondy said. "Don't let it burn down, man. It's precious stuff. Every puff is a dream."

I inhaled my first joint, filling my lungs, and passed it back to Blondy. The sweet smell of the smoke hung in the humid air. I was worried about the sergeant. Blondy paid him no attention. He puffed and passed it. So it went. With each drag, I kept my eyes on Sergeant Stone. He never looked our way.

"Don't worry about the old man," Blondy said. "He doesn't indulge but he understands. He's figured the odds. He doesn't want to get bagged in the back."

I looked nervously at Blondy.

"Relax, man. Your adrenaline's working against it. Here.

19

Take off. Fly, man. It's your best fucking weapon against Charlie. Believe me." He gave me the joint.

I closed my eyes and sucked it hungrily. And again before I returned it. I began to feel just fine. The trees shimmered in the morning light and the birdcalls suddenly filtered through to me. I separated each call and focused on the most melodious. My head danced to their song. I remembered the times in basic when I'd passed up the offers of a joint. The drill sergeants were tough about it and made life miserable. One guy even baked a cake with grass and got busted for it. I played it safe then and regretted it now. I could have floated through basic on a cloud, like I was floating now. The VC couldn't get me. I'd just fly away. Fly away in the blue.

I noticed big, black Corporal Thomas, still standing, looking down that trail and sucking on a butt. He was swaying lightly to an inner rhythm. He's got his, I thought. I wondered how many days he had to go. Maybe, I thought, maybe he's my lucky asshole after Blondy.

I looked at Blondy taking a last drag. He lived as the joint died on his lips. Letting it fall to the ground, he smiled at me. "How about it, Glass? Charlie ain't worrying you, is he?"

I laughed for the first time that morning. "Only if he's smoking grass."

Blondy nodded very slowly. "He don't need no grass. He's got purpose."

"I don't want him to kill me," I said. "And I don't want to kill him."

"Don't think about killing. It'll come by itself." His old eyes narrowed. "You just do what the old man tells you and you'll be all right. He's outguessed Charlie for sixteen months. He's got a lot of mileage to protect."

"What about Corporal Thomas? How much mileage's he got?"

"I don't know. He does a solo. He even flies alone. Look at him. He's sucking his joint and still sniffing that trail like it's going somewhere. It's only going down, man. I want to go up up and away." He wafted his hand toward

20

the trees and the sky. "I can taste it. Just thirty-two more days and I'll leave this asshole for paradise."

"Where's that?" I asked.

"Cuntsville, the U.S. of A." He clutched his groin and shouted, "Yah-hoo, Blondy Cooper's ready on the firing line."

I was there with him when Sergeant Stone tuned us in. "Okay, you jockeys. Mount up." He got to his feet.

We all rose with him. Corporal Thomas danced to one side to let the sergeant enter the trail. We descended into the valley, only now, my pack felt lighter and my spirit soared. Even the brutal heat didn't bother me until we reached the valley floor.

O

It was nine o'clock when we reached the bottom of the trail. With the slow climb down from the plateau behind us and the flat open valley ahead of us, Sergeant Stone called another halt. While we rested, he clambered a few feet into a tree nearby to survey the terrain. Corporal Thomas stayed close to him.

The trail down ended abruptly at the base and there were no worn trails visible in the valley. Blondy told me that patrols passing through before us had probably taken their own fresh routes and the dense high grass had swallowed up their course. That was all to the good, he said, because out in the open, trails were tempting to use but potentially very dangerous. While you could make better time on a path through the undergrowth, the VC stalked them well. They know the terrain, Blondy said, and we don't. They plant the mines and we step on them. They set up the ambush and we get ambushed. They do the sniping and we get picked off. And they, almost always, choose the time and place of an encounter.

"It's their show," Blondy said, regarding me soberly, "and we come to it. So the old man's up in that tree scouting a way through that field where Charlie ain't likely to be. But don't ask me how he's going to decide."

Blondy scanned the high grass ahead of us. "It looks

so peaceful, don't it? Like a fucking cornfield in Iowa. What could hurt you out there? Maybe nothing. My guess is it's safe. I'm more worried about crossing that river. That's where Charlie's likely to be. He can get a clear shot at us on that river and we got to hold our rifles over our heads above the water line. He likes that. It makes us easy pickings."

"You're scaring the shit out of me," I said.

The redheaded Raggedy Andy doll, lying on his pack a few feet away, laughed tightly. "He's full of shit, kid. Tune him out."

"Fuck you, Andy," Blondy said. "How much time you got?"

"Two hundred days and five hours and three rivers, including that one up ahead. I been across it and back. It's real shallow. You can walk on it like you was Jesus Christ."

"You been through this field, then?" Blondy asked.

"Going and coming."

"Does the old man know that?"

"I wasn't with the old man."

"Then why don't you tell him the route you took, ass-hole?"

"Because that's where Charlie might be."

"He wasn't there before."

"Yeah. He wasn't. You going to give us an affidavit he ain't there now? The old man's leading this patrol, not me."

"And you follow, huh?"

"By the book. I'm just a plain simple corporal, Private Cooper."

"Up yours."

The redhead smiled, mopped his sweaty brow and closed his eyes.

The heat was oppressive and it was only early morning. By noon the valley would be a furnace. The Vietnamese were better able to endure it. Their straw hats were a lot cooler than our helmets. The heat was also a natural part of their lives. We weren't conditioned to it and the armor of a GI was designed for protection against bullets, not the sun.

My body wilted in my clothes and I could feel those sweet, potheaded dreams rapidly escaping through my sweating pores. What a fucking place to be. What a fucking place to fight a war. It didn't make sense to me. Why am I here? I distracted myself by thinking about the redhead. He interested me. He had three rivers behind him. Blondy had called him Andy and I wondered if that was his real name. Suddenly, the names the sergeant had ticked off in the mess registered fresh—Cooper, Thomas, Doll. The redhead had to be Doll. I smiled to myself. Andy Doll, skinny, freckle-faced, red-haired. No wonder he could walk on water. He was something else.

"Corporal Andy Doll," I said aloud.

The redhead opened his eyes. "That's me."

"It sure is," I said and I grinned like an ass.

Raggedy Andy was beginning to look like a good bet to make it. Not counting Corporal Thomas, doing his solo, I was surrounded by nearly three years of combat experience. That was comforting to a guy with a total of two days of tent time and four hours of patrol.

○

We started through the high grass taking a southwesterly route with Sergeant Stone leading, Corporal Thomas next and then Doll, Blondy and me. We kept five yards apart. It wasn't too bad at first except that I was feeling a bit lonely. The grasses screened us off and I could only see Blondy ahead of me. I kept my eyes fixed on his shiny blond hair bobbing in the shimmering light. A couple of times I had the thought that he was the only one out there with me and once, when I lost sight of him, I quickened my pace. His bobbing head came into view and after that I closed the gap to three yards. If anything got him it might get me but that lonely feeling was more frightening.

After a while it seemed like we'd been marching through that field for days. The sun beat on us. It had to be a hundred and twenty degrees. My body flowed sweat that caked white on my arms. I kept popping down salt pills until my tongue was so coated I couldn't collect enough saliva to spit. Worst of all, the grasses grew so dense their blades chopped like knives on my arms. And once, when I brushed the grass away from my face, my hand touched the barrel of my M-16. It burned like a hot stove. I wondered if the heat affected the accuracy of the weapon and I kept it lowered to avoid the direct rays of the sun.

There was no talk as we moved forward. No one to talk to. I had to endure my misery in silence when I wanted to bitch about the lead soles of my boots, the rucksack loaded with two hundred pounds of rock boring a hole in my back, the flack vest squeezing my chest like a cylinder of hot pipe. I was the well-equipped fighting man with no fight in me. If I had met Charlie in his black pajamas at that moment, I'd have had it. Or so I thought. Fortunately, we made it safely to the river.

Sergeant Stone had led us to the only spot where the tall grass came right to the river's edge so we still had the cover of the grass from which to study a way across. How the sergeant found it through the flat maze of that field I don't know but my respect for him rose another notch.

We squatted close together on the ground to rest. I was relieved to have that field of knives behind me and to be near the others again. In the hour it had taken us to cross the field I had felt isolated. After catching his breath, Sergeant Stone removed his helmet and cautiously filled it with river water, extending only his hand beyond the protection of the grass. He poured the water over his head and put his helmet back on. We passed our helmets forward to him to be filled. The water was warm but refreshing. As it ran down my face and trickled under my shirt I couldn't remember anything feeling so good. I wanted desperately to strip to my skin and dive into that river. It was only six feet away from our burning hell—flowing, gurgling, beckoning to me to take its pleasure. It was a suicidal desire I resisted. It would happen again and again, that juxtaposition of physical extremes in Vietnam. It worked an insidious torture on the body and mind.

My lightheaded thoughts of cooling myself in the river were interrupted by the business at hand: how to get across it. At the point we were at it looked a lot deeper than Andy Doll had told us. The sergeant and Corporal Thomas were discussing the merits of heading south or north to find a shallower spot when Blondy volunteered the services of Doll.

"Doll's been across it before. Maybe he can help out."

"What about it, Doll?" the sergeant asked.

"I don't recognize this part. I was much further south. It was real shallow there. We walked across it. It didn't hardly cover the tops of our boots."

"How much further south?"

"I don't rightly know, sarge. Could have been a mile, maybe two, maybe more."

"That's no help," the sergeant said. "The ravine's north of us on the other side. We can't detour that much. We ain't got the time and we'd be potshots strolling along this fucking river. We got to find a spot along here."

Doll shrugged indifferently. "Sorry I can't help you, sarge. We weren't heading for the ravine that day."

"Yeah. You run into Charlie that day?"

"Nope."

"What the hell were you looking for?"

"Charlie."

"Then you fucked up."

"No sir, sarge. We went, we looked, we didn't find nothing so we came back."

"You fucked up," the sergeant repeated.

"How come?"

"'Cause Charlie wanted you to find nothing. That's how come."

"He found nothing, too, sarge. We got home safe."

"Smart ass. He could a been watching you all the time, biding his time."

"Yeah. I'm glad he bided till we got our asses out of there."

"You ain't here to save your ass, Doll. You're here to find Charlie and kill him."

"I do my best, sarge."

"You fucking better." The sergeant broke it off and turned his attention back to the river. "What do you think, Thomas?" He pointed south. "It looks like shoals up ahead and the grass is thick on the other side. It'll give us quick cover."

"Whatever you say, sarge," Corporal Thomas answered.

The sergeant stared at him for a moment. "Okay. Let's move. Keep the same space as we go along the bank. If Charlie opens up scramble into the grass. And keep that fucking radio dry, Thomas."

"Yes sir."

Sergeant Stone got to his feet in a crouch. The rest of us copied him. This is it, I thought. Charlie's waiting out there. I felt the sweat oozing down from my crotch. I knew one thing for sure. I wasn't going to piss in my pants. Every drop of water in my body was gushing out of my pores.

Sergeant Stone started slowly forward along the bank.

"Hold it, sarge," Doll whispered. "Get back here." The sharp authority in his voice drew the sergeant back.

"What is it?"

"Charlie." Doll pointed north.

Through the swaying shield of grass we could see a small black figure a hundred yards off, approaching slowly along the riverbank.

"Get down and don't move," the sergeant said. He dropped to his knees and raised his M-16. The others did the same. I wanted to crawl into the earth but I forced myself to aim my rifle.

"Don't fire," the sergeant said. "Let him come."

With the five of us holding our rifles on him, the black figure came on slowly. We were so still I became aware of every sound in the valley—the birdcalls, the water lapping, the grasses swishing. The sweat ran into my eyes, forcing me to blink. I had Charlie in my sight but I couldn't hold the barrel steady. I began to shiver. My head reeled. I wanted to get up and run. I wanted Charlie to disappear. I prayed he would turn and go back down the river. But he kept on coming.

When he was fifty yards from us, I got my first good look at the enemy. "It's only a kid," I blurted tensely.

"Shut up!" the old man rasped through his teeth. "He's going to walk right into us. Maybe we can take this motherfucker alive. Don't fire unless he breaks for it."

My M-16 weighed a hundred pounds in my sweating hands. I lowered it against my chest. It wasn't going to take five of us to kill a ten-year-old boy in black pajamas. That's all he was in my eyes—a kid wandering idly along a quiet river in a quiet valley, squishing the river mud between his toes. I kept my eyes on him. He seemed unaware of any danger. Every few steps he bent down to scoop the river water into his face.

Beside me, Blondy and the others squatted motionless, their rifles fixed on the boy. They looked totally unreal to me. I was unreal to myself. Only four months ago I had been in an orphanage filling out forms to join the army. And here I was lying in wait to participate in the killing of a ten-year-old boy. Did he threaten my life? Was he my enemy? Two hours ago I was a pothead. Was I still a pothead, hallucinating? The answer I came up with was no. I'm here in this steaming valley in Vietnam. I know because the sweat is pouring out of my body. And that boy is a boy. He lives here and he takes walks along his river. Why not? But doesn't he know there's a war going on? I chuckled foolishly but quickly stifled it. Four men with automatic rifles were not amused and they were just as real as the heat of the sun, the flowing river, the swaying grasses and that kid squishing the mud between his toes. But man, if I wasn't crazy, somebody, somewhere, pulling the strings, was.

O

And the kid came on. The river absorbed his attention. He took off his straw hat and drew it through the water and then pulled it out and examined it. He repeated the action several times. A boy trying to scoop small fish into his net. Each time his face registered disappointment but he continued undiscouraged. The closer he got to us, the more frail he became. A thin, scrawny boy in billowing pajamas. Five yards from us, he stopped to contemplate the high grass that blocked his passage along the shore. A frown of indecision furrowed his small face. In that moment, our stillness seemed unendurable. Carefully, the sergeant lowered his M-16 to the ground. The others kept their bead on the boy. He came forward, deciding to cut through the grass rather than wade into the river. He came straight through the high grass into the thick arms of Sergeant Stone, who sprang up to clutch him. "You motherfucker," the old man exclaimed gleefully. He pulled the boy down onto the ground and pressed his hand tightly around his throat and straddled him. It happened so quickly there had been no opportunity for the boy to cry out and the sergeant's fingers on his throat now guaranteed his silence. The others pressed around the sergeant. Reluctantly, I joined them, unable to resist an inexplicable fascination. The sergeant was exultant about his catch. The boy stared into our faces, his eyes full of fear. The sudden change in his circumstances was incomprehensible to him.

"What're you going to do with him, sarge?" Corporal Thomas asked.

Sergeant Stone responded by pulling a knife from his belt with his free hand. "I'm going to slit his throat." He raised the knife so the boy could see it and then he held it against the boy's chin. The boy closed his eyes tightly. Tears squeezed out through his lids.

"Wait, sarge. Maybe he knows this river and can get us across," Corporal Thomas said.

The old man scowled. "You speak gook, Thomas?"

"No sir."

"I do, sarge," Doll said.

"You kidding me, smart ass?"

"I wouldn't kid you, sarge. I'm a language student. I picked up some Vietnamese."

"You?"

"Sure as you're the leader of this patrol. Ease up on his tonsils and I'll talk to him."

"He just might open his yap and bring this whole fucking valley of VC down on us. You think of that?"

"I don't rightly think so, sarge. Not with that knife at his gullet. Corporal Thomas might have something. Ain't we supposed to pick up all the info we can? It's worth a try."

The old man hesitated and then nodded. "Okay. Try it. But one peep out of him and he's a dead gook." The sergeant raised his knife above the boy's head and released his hold on his throat.

"Talk to him, Doll. Find out who he is and where he's from."

Corporal Doll leaned forward over the boy and spoke haltingly. It sounded like gibberish to me but the boy's eyes responded knowingly. When Doll finished, the boy answered in a gush.

"What's he say?" the old man asked.

"He lives south of here in a hamlet. He's hungry. He was trying to catch fish in the river."

"Shit," the sergeant said. "Ask him if the VC control his village."

Doll questioned the boy at length and he answered at length, never taking his eyes from the knife held over him.

"Yeah?"

"The whole valley's crawling with VC," Doll said.

"Including him," the sergeant said.

Doll shook his head. "He's just a village kid. He says

Charlie stays across the river during the day and only comes over at night to get food and keep them villagers scared."

"Yeah. And you believe that gook shit?"

"I believe him, sarge. He's under the knife."

"Shit. He's a fucking VC. He's wearing them black pajamas, ain't he? They're always using kids to scout for them."

"He ain't armed, sarge."

"That don't mean nothing."

Corporal Thomas cut in: "Ask him does he know where Charlie holes up across the river. Ask him does he know if we can cross up ahead."

Doll looked at the sergeant.

"Ask him."

Doll cackled away and the kid answered slowly this time. He was eager to cooperate.

"He says Charlie's holed up in that tangle of trees at the foot of the hills on the other side."

"The ravine?"

"Yeah. He says it's a cobweb of caves."

"See, sarge," Corporal Thomas said, beaming. "He's a real help."

The sergeant's face brightened. "Did you ask him if we can walk across the river?"

Doll nodded. "Up ahead. Them shoals you seen. It's shallow there."

"And Charlie's there, too, I'll bet."

"I don't think so. He says Charlie stays in the tangle. He don't come out except at night. That's why the kid was walking along the river. He done it before and he don't want to run into Charlie any more'n we do."

"Shit," the sergeant said. "Just ask him if he'll lead us over them shoals."

Doll questioned the boy and pointed up the river. The kid shook his head severely. When he spoke, his eyes were fixed on the old man.

"See," the sergeant exclaimed. "Charlie's waiting right there, isn't he?"

"The kid didn't say that, sarge. He's afraid to cross the river. He says the VC's there but he don't know where except the ravine. But we got to cross it so I think them shoals is our best bet. Like you said, we can get across fast and the bushes is thick on the other side."

"Yeah. That's what I said. And we better get moving."

"What about the kid?" Corporal Thomas asked. "We taking him with us?"

"Shit no. We got all we need from him."

"You going to let him go?"

The sergeant answered with a quick deep thrust of his knife across the boy's throat. A horrible, gurgling cry rose from the boy's mouth. Blood spurted up in a torrent from his throat and washed over his chest, spattering the sergeant's legs. The old man raised himself on his haunches. The boy shuddered over on his side and lay still. We were all stunned into silence.

"Okay, let's get moving," the sergeant said. He darted through the grass toward the riverbank. The others scrambled after him, anxious to get away. I moved more slowly, stepping around the dead boy. Blood still flowed from his throat. I lagged after Blondy. The taste of nausea filled my mouth and a spasm of the dry heaves shuddered through my body but fear propelled me forward.

○

Without the cover of the grass, we proceeded swiftly along the riverbank toward the shoals. I tried to concentrate on the serious business at hand, telling myself that Charlie was somewhere out there watching us, waiting to ambush us. But my mind whirled with images of the business behind us. I kept hearing the boy's scream and seeing the blood pouring out of his mouth. My legs wobbled. I stumbled on a rock and went sprawling flat, striking the ground hard at the river's edge. River water splashed over my face. I wanted to close my eyes and just lie there— to escape my reality. But my rifle was under me, pressing into my chest. It mustn't get wet. Instinctively, I rolled on my back, holding my M-16 above me. I looked up at the serene, pale blue sky. The small face of Blondy cut into it. He looked very old.

"You okay?"

I sat up and he pulled me to my feet. "Yeah."

"Keep moving, man."

He turned away before I could ask him about the kid. I straggled after him. I had a million questions to ask but no one to hear them.

Fifty, seventy-five, a hundred yards from the murdered boy—it seemed like an eternity of space—we reached the shallows where the riverbed rose up and the water bubbled over the sandy bottom. We bunched up around Sergeant Stone. He looked untroubled by what he had done and concerned only with the immediate situation. He was scanning the opposite bank. It looked peaceful.

"Okay," he said. "We can't sit out here. I'll go across first. You follow in line. We'll collect in the bullrushes on the other side and study the map before moving ahead. Watch your footing." He started across the shoals. Corporal Thomas gave him five long yards and followed. Andy Doll was next and then Blondy. I stayed right on Blondy's ass.

The river was no more than thirty yards wide at that point. The riverbed was firm but I concentrated on each step. I didn't want to stumble again. I wasn't going to fuck up. At the front of my mind, I thought about the dead boy and I knew at that moment I had to get an accounting for him and for me.

I was picking my way in midstream, oblivious to any danger that might lie ahead, when an immense explosion shattered the stillness. Steel pellets sang through the air all around me.

"Claymores!" Corporal Thomas shouted.

In front of me, the others had dropped to their knees in the water. I remained standing, stunned, staring ahead. On the bank, fifteen yards off, Sergeant Stone lay in a bundle face down, his arms clutching his belly. He didn't move or make a sound.

I got down on my knees in the river behind Blondy. Ahead of us, Doll was down so low his face was almost in the river but he held his M-16 above the water line. Thomas was five yards from the old man. He started crawling toward him.

"Hold it, Thomas," Doll called. "You want to blow us all up?"

Thomas looked back. "We gotta get the old man."

"We gotta get our asses into those bushes before we're lying there with him." Doll scrambled to his feet and hurried into the deeper water on the right. "Come on."

Blondy and I responded to his command. In seconds we were on the bank and into the bushes. Corporal Thomas flopped in behind us.

"Now we can plan strategy," Doll said. "Where we ain't exposed."

"And now I'm in command," Thomas said.

"I guess you are," Doll said. "The old man's sure in no condition if he's still alive."

"That's what we're going to find out," Thomas said.

"Who's we?"

"Like you, Doll. Crawl out there and see."

"Not me." Doll squinted. He held his rifle in front of him, his finger on the trigger. "Charlie's just waiting for the first bastard dumb enough to show. I seen it happen."

"You gonna let him die out there?"

"You asking my advice, Thomas?"

"Yeah, smart ass."

"Call out to him. If he's alive, he'll answer. Then we can risk getting him back in here. If he's dead we can't help him no more."

"He's right, Thomas," Blondy said.

"Nobody asking you."

"I got three hundred and thirty-three days. How much you got, Thomas?"

"Shut your ass. Okay, Doll. Start calling."

"Yes sir, corporal." Doll kept his face straight. He crawled forward toward the edge of the bushes, a few feet from us. I estimated that we were about ten yards from where the sergeant lay but we couldn't see him through the thick grass.

"Hey sarge," Doll called out.

No answer.

Then louder. "Sarge, you there?"

Silence.

"He could be unconscious," Thomas said.

"Yeah," Doll said. He backed into our cover.

"We got to get to him," Thomas said. He looked worried. "Even if he's dead."

"How come?"

"He's got the map on him."

"Ain't you got a map?"

"I told you he's got the fucking map."

"The hell with the map."

"How we going to find the ravine, smart ass?"

"Fuck the ravine."

"You going to tell them that back at headquarters? We got a job to do."

"You're leading this patrol, Thomas. I'll follow wherever you lead. I just ain't going out there by my lonesome to search a dead man. Not while Charlie's sweating us out."

"How you know Charlie's waiting? A mine got the old man, not Charlie."

"Charlie put that mine there. Right at the edge of them shoals. He figured we'd come across the river there and we did. Now I figure he's sitting watch on that spot. It's standard gook procedure."

"Shit. You figured like the rest of us that the shoals was the place to cross. I heard you."

"Sure. And I was wrong."

"But this time you're right, huh?"

"If I ain't why don't you crawl out there and find out?"

"You yellow motherfucker," Thomas said. "I ought to—"

"Don't fuck with me, corporal," Doll said. "I just ain't risking my ass for no dead man. It don't make no sense."

"This whole fucking war don't make no sense but we're fighting it, ain't we?"

"Not stupidly if I can help it."

Thomas pointed his finger at Doll's face. "When we get back I'm putting you on report for refusing to obey orders. Now get your ass out of my way. I'm going out and get that map." He pushed past Doll and started crawling through the grass.

"Hey, how about leaving the radio? If Charlie gets you you won't be needing it."

"You'll just have to come and get it." And he disappeared.

"Dumb bastard," Doll said. He looked at Blondy and then me for agreement. He didn't get it.

We sat there in silence listening for some sound of Corporal Thomas. We heard nothing. Minutes passed. "He must be there by now," Blondy said. "Maybe it's—"

Automatic rifle fire startled us. It sounded like a single burst from the direction Thomas had gone only it came from more than ten yards away.

Doll bolted up straight on his knees, and Blondy too, their M-16's cocked and pointing. I aimed in the same direction. All I could see was the grass, and through it the sky. They were not my enemy or were they? All I could hear was the sound of my own breathing, fast, nervous.

"That was Charlie," Doll whispered. "They must have got Thomas. The dumb bastard. I warned him not to go out there. I warned him. It's not my fault." He felt guilty and I liked him for that.

"What do we do?" Blondy asked.

"We sweat and wait until we know how many's out there. That was only a burst from a single AK. Goddamnit, that wise ass should have left us the fucking radio. We sure could use some support." All the time Doll was talking he kept his sight down the barrel of his M-16.

"They got to know we're here," Blondy said.

"Yeah, like we know they're there. But maybe there's only one of them sitting watch on them mines and waiting

35

to pick us off one at a time. It wouldn't be the first time old Charlie did that. One time a single VC kept a whole platoon pinned down. They thought they was surrounded and called in a couple of gunships. When they cleared the area all they found was one dead gook stuffed in a rat's hole." Doll turned briefly to grin at us. "Two gunships and a whole platoon to waste one gook. You just know that platoon lieutenant got his ass—"

There was a second burst of gunfire. Closer this time. Bullets thudded to the left of our position. In the same instant, Doll and Blondy whipped their rifles to the left at the sound of scurrying footsteps. I froze like a statue.

"Don't fire!" Corporal Thomas's huge body loomed above us in the grass and then crashed at our feet.

"You damn near got your head blown off," Doll rasped.

Thomas raised his head. "Yeah, going and coming," he panted, and he sat up.

"What happened out there?"

"I'll tell you after we get that gook." He pointed in the direction of the gunfire. "See that tree to the right, twenty-five yards off?"

"Yeah."

"The fucker's in it about fifteen feet off the ground."

"I can't see through the grass."

"You don't have to. He's there all by his lonesome. All we got to do is spray him through the grass."

"How do you know he's alone?"

" 'Cause he used me for his fucking target practice. If there were more I'da been long gone from this craphole. And you'da know'd it, too. He's sitting deathwatch on the old man, like you said. He can see the whole river from up there. He must have seen us scramble in here. Only he ain't about to take us all on. He figured to stack us up neat like cordwood. But now *he's* sweating."

"He could be long gone by now."

Thomas shook his head. "He don't know I seen him up there. Let's line up but stay low. When I open up, fire through the tips of the grass. Give him the whole clip."

We lined up abreast and aimed our rifles. Thomas started firing, then Doll and Blondy. The roar was deafening. I squeezed the trigger. Nothing happened. My safety was on. I released it as they emptied their magazines. A piercing scream mixed with the gunfire. I never got off a single round. I thought of the old man lying out there. He'd never know I'd fucked up. The others loaded fresh clips, unaware that I hadn't fired. Thomas raised himself slowly and peered over the top of the grass, his M-16 at the ready. Grinning, he lowered his rifle. "Take a look, man. He's still in that tree and he ain't coming down no more."

We stood up. The silence seemed greater than before the gunfire. The tree stood alone in the field of grass. It was a strange sight—a lone sentinel in that open field, a whim of nature. And it bore a strange burden. The body of the dead man was caught in its lower branches where it had fallen violently. The rifle, dangling from a strap around the neck, swayed gently with a muted life of its own.

"The AK is mine," Corporal Thomas said.

"You can have the rifle," Doll said. "I'm taking the ears, man. We got a kill."

O

We sat there in the bushes for maybe fifteen minutes, smoking, talking, letting the tensions ease off and giving ourselves time to be certain the area was clear. Thomas told us what had happened to him. Doll listened without interrupting but his smug expression punctuated several points in Thomas's tale.

The corporal had crawled out to the body of the old man without difficulty. He found Sergeant Stone dead as his name, his body oozing from a thousand punctures and his guts spewed out on the ground. He rolled the sergeant over to search his pockets for the map when the gook opened up with his AK.

"I practically climbed inside the old man's body," Thomas said. "It was the only fucking cover I had. Man,

I was scared shitless but I didn't move a toenail. I played dead. I knew the gook still had half a clip before reloading. I opened one eye and spotted him shifting in that tree. I figured he wouldn't come down to check me out because he knew you guys were in the bushes. I prayed you'd open up on him and I'd make a break for it. But nothing happened."

"We thought you bought it," Blondy said. "We didn't know where the hell he was and how many were with him."

"Yeah. I figured as much but I couldn't lie there all day. I waited until I heard him move again in the branches and then I bolted in here. Caught the fucker by surprise. I guess the old man took the rest of the clip." He shook his head thoughtfully. "It didn't mean nothing to him no more. He saved my fucking life, that dead old man."

No one said anything. We dragged on our butts. I wondered how old the old man was. A lot older than me, I thought. Maybe twenty-three. But I didn't ask.

Doll finally broke the silence, all business: "Did you get the map?"

"No. But it ain't going nowhere."

"Yeah. Let's get it and make tracks. We ain't doing no good here."

"Right." Thomas paused. "Maybe I better call into headquarters and report."

"What've you got to report?" Doll asked.

"Our position. The minefield. The old man. And we encountered Charlie, didn't we?"

"One gook. That's all so far. That ain't exactly the location of enemy forces. I'd hold it up until we really run into something."

"Maybe you're right," Thomas admitted reluctantly. "Let's go."

We left our cover, cautiously at first, then more relaxed. The sergeant was right there on the riverbank where I'd seen him, only now he was turned over on his back. His belly was sliced open like he'd been carved with

38

a blunt meat cleaver. When I saw that he had nothing left between his legs I turned away. Thomas took the map from the body, emptied the rest of the pockets into his rucksack and rolled the body over face down. Doll took the old man's ammunition belt and M-16. He removed the clip and threw the rifle into the river.

"Let's pull him into the bushes," Doll said. "If the gooks run across him here, they'll strip him naked. If he's still in the bushes when we come back, maybe we can call in a chopper to take him out."

We towed the corpse of Sergeant Stone—I never found out his first name—into the high grass near the edge of the river. Then we moved on to the next corpse, asleep in the tree.

Thomas reached up and cut the sling of the AK and grasped the rifle for himself. Doll contemplated the situation. He wanted Charlie's ears but the body was slumped on a limb six feet above the ground and he couldn't reach the head. He considered pulling Charlie to the ground but decided against it. He liked the idea of Charlie squatting dead in that tree. It made a good land-mark to guide us on the way home. He settled for a finger of Charlie's right hand, which he could reach without dif-ficulty. He sawed off the middle finger with his knife. It took some effort to cut through the bone but Charlie never said a word.

O

The map showed our position on the river to be due east of the ravine. A path ran from the mined area at the river straight west through the grass toward a line of trees. We stayed off it and thrashed our way through the high, thick grass. The sun was directly overhead, beating on our helmets. My head throbbed from the heat but the grass was more aggravating. I hacked it at eye-level to keep my face clear of its cutting edges. I stayed close to Blondy. I didn't want to get separated from him. He was the only one who showed any concern for me. The other

39

two were strictly watching out for themselves. I remembered the rule I'd learned in basic: the mission comes first; your men second; then you. Bullshit! Doll had taught me the truth: your own ass first, then your buddy and fuck the mission. That's the way it was on that first patrol and that's the way it was for the rest of my year in Vietnam. You ask anybody who was there in '68 and '69. If they tell you differently, they're lying. With the electric chair possibly facing me for what I did, I'm beyond lies. They can't help me.

I cannot escape the circumstances under which I'm writing. The bars of my cell are three feet away and my jailer stands vigil as I write. At times it's difficult for me to concentrate on that first patrol and all that followed. It all seems so unreal to me now. My cell and my jailer and understanding even if I may not live to know it. So under my trial are my only reality. Yet I am in serious need of the stern gaze of my jailer, who cannot conceal his hatred for me, I go on. Fortunately, he is powerless to stop me.

5.

We reached the line of trees without trouble. It had been slow, heavy going through the grass and we were dog-tired from the heat and the mental strain of staying on the alert for the enemy. Until we had encountered the boy on the riverbank the patrol had been routine. There had been only physical hardship. But, for me, the killing of the boy had sparked a tension that was far more debilitating than the physical discomfort. And the quick death of the old man and my first encounter with the enemy had increased that tension. I was knotted with fear of the enemy and a growing uneasiness with the members of my patrol.

Once we had crossed that river, we were in VC territory—in the enemy ball park, only it was more a game of hide-and-seek than baseball. In the orphanage, when my friends hid and I had to find them I tensed up waiting for the unexpected. But when I hid, I was relaxed because I could watch the seeker from the protection of my hiding place. In this war, I learned quickly that I was always the seeker while the enemy hid and watched and picked the moment of surprise. In that long year, I never got used to it and I was never more up-tight than on that first patrol.

When we finally halted at the tree line and flopped down to rest and eat in the shade, I was a fist of nerves. Though I hadn't had anything but a cup of coffee for more than seven hours, I could barely eat two mouthfuls of my C-rations. But I drank almost half the water in my canteen, letting some of it spill down my chin and under my shirt. It soothed me inside and out.

The others ate with less difficulty, particularly Corporal Thomas, whose appetite never flagged no matter the situation. Blondy sensed my tension and offered me the only cure for it under the circumstances—a fresh joint, all for myself. I was very grateful. By the time I finished it, I was limp as a rag doll and keenly alert. I observed the other Doll, Corporal Andy, with interest. He was studying the rest of us, a look of contempt on his face. He didn't indulge in the joys of grass and he had no use for us potheads. We made him uneasy. Corporal Thomas was out of it, doing his solo, his head resting against a tree trunk and his eyes closed to this world.

Blondy punched my arm good-naturedly and chuckled at me. "Thirty-one and a half days and then paradise."

I laughed.

"You keep flying like that," Doll said, "and a gook bullet will send you to paradise right here."

"You want a drag, Andy boy? It'll loosen you up."

"I ain't no pothead."

"You sure ain't. You're a trophy hunter."

"What's that mean?"

"What'd you do with Charlie's finger? Plug your asshole with it?"

"Don't push it, pothead. You might need me before this day's over."

"Like the old man needed you?"

"The old man's in paradise."

"Amen."

"Knock it off," Corporal Thomas said.

He took out the map and spread it on the ground. He and Doll studied it and discussed the route to take through

42

the woods to the ravine. Thomas made a tentative sugges-
tion to bear south and cut back to the right to approach
the ravine from the side. Doll objected because it would
add an hour to our time through the woods. He was for
taking a straight line to the ravine. Thomas was against
it but could give no reason. Neither of them knew where
the enemy was in those woods, if he was there, but
Thomas persisted for his way and he wanted Doll to agree
with his strategy as he had done with Sergeant Stone.
That was the role of the number two man, which Doll
had now assumed. But Doll couldn't "yessir" Thomas. He
contested Thomas's position without openly contesting his
leadership, but Thomas knew enough to know that that
was at the root of it. And he was still smarting from the
initiatives Doll had already taken since the old man had
gotten blown apart. He was determined to get Doll to accept
his leadership and Doll was equally determined to question
it. The contest was uneven. Thomas had only his gut courage
going for him. It was no match for Doll's shrewdness.

Listening to them bicker, I thought that if I had to
choose which one to follow, it would be Doll. I had no
heart for the values of Corporal Andy Doll. He was an
instinctive killer but he was cautious, a survivor, and I
wanted desperately to survive.

By now, less than eight hours out on my first patrol, I
had witnessed the absurd death of a boy, the absurd death
of his murderer and, yes, the absurd death of an unfamiliar
enemy we familiarly called Charlie. It all seemed like a
terrible madness to me, and the more so because I was
ready to follow the instincts of a stranger who had sawed
off the finger of a dead man.

That was the kind of shit I had to swallow that day
and all the days of my war. I remembered reading once
that a man did not have to eat shit to know it didn't taste
good, and I believed it. I no longer believe it. It depends
on the man.

At that moment, if it had been in my power, I'd have
put a general—no, the President—at the head of a patrol.

43

What did the President know about eating the shit of his war from the rear area of the Oval Room? I wanted him to experience the terrible taste in my mouth.

Such were my potheaded thoughts as I clung to the absurdity of my life in that quiet, tree-shaded glen where little men in black pajamas were waiting somewhere to kill me. They had cause. I had nothing.

O

The discussion of our route through the woods ended with Thomas grudgingly accepting Doll's view but only because we were behind our schedule. We took a straight course to the ravine. Doll volunteered to lead and this time Thomas readily agreed. He was really more comfortable being the number two man and it was less dangerous. The lead man always ran the greatest risk. Sergeant Stone had demonstrated that. But I think Thomas had another purpose. If we fucked up in any way, he figured it would be on Doll's head. What the poor bastard didn't consider was that he was officially in command of the patrol and whatever happened would be his responsibility. Smoking grass didn't sharpen his mind, only his senses. And as it happened, that was what he needed.

The blades of light stabbing through the trees created a series of screens, making it difficult to see ahead. The glare tormented my eyes. I clenched my teeth and concentrated my vision on the woods ahead of me. My mind was clear but I had the jitters. It was the effects of the grass wearing off. Still, I plodded steadily forward determined not to let the light and shadows in the woods weaken me. The trees were full of birds trilling their individual songs. They beat too loudly on my ears, increasing the tension in my skull. I couldn't shut them out. The grass had sharpened my hearing. It had the same effect on Thomas. At almost every step his head would dart to the left or right at the sound of the leaves fluttering or the call of a bird. He was jumpy and it was contagious. The hum of insects around my head startled me and the

44

sound of our footsteps beat loudly. Blondy, too, reacted to the noises in the woods.

Only Doll seemed undisturbed by the sounds. He walked steadily on, getting farther ahead of us until Thomas called to him to slow up. He stopped to look back. A screeching bird flew across our path and disappeared in the foliage. The sound of a twig snapping came from our right. We all heard it and stopped in our tracks. It came from behind a thicket. Something stirred in the bramble. Thomas reacted the quickest, dropping flat on his chest. Blondy and I fell beside him. Doll stayed on his feet in a crouch, his M-16 fixed on the bramble. A loud crackling sound came from it. Doll opened up, spraying his gunfire in an arc across the bramble. Thomas let go with a short burst. Blondy and I held our fire, waiting to see something to shoot at. We heard a strange snorting and groaning. The bramble shook like it was alive. Doll fired off his clip. A water buffalo came crashing through the thicket. It wobbled unsteadily, blood pouring from its masive head. Thomas emptied his magazine right into its eyes. The monstrous animal toppled to the earth six feet from us. Its spindly legs twitched in a final spasm of death just like the legs of the boy on the riverbank. Our feeling of relief was enormous.

Doll walked up to the animal and kicked its bloody snout with the toe of his boot. He grinned. "One dead gook and one dead gook buffalo for our side."

"And one dead boy," I said, unable to contain myself for the first time that day.

"That's right. I forgot about him. Two dead gooks. Not bad."

"You going to cut off the buffalo's ears, Doll?" Blondy asked. "It ain't got fingers."

"Fuck you, pothead."

"I just thought for your trophy collection."

"I'm warning you not to push it."

"Yeah," Thomas said. He was on his feet, loading a fresh clip. "Let's go. We made enough noise around here."

45

We moved through the woods more cautiously, worrying that our gunfire had aroused Charlie. Our worries came to naught. We reached the edge of the woods at two o'clock without encountering a sign of the enemy. Ahead of us was a paddy field, and beyond it the ravine at the base of the western hills. We stayed in the cover of the trees and calculated our next move. We knew that the VC were lodged in the hills and could mortar anything that moved across that paddy. What we didn't know and were on orders to find out was the extent of VC activity in the ravine. Were they moving down from the hills? For what purpose?

Looking across the no man's land of that paddy, I didn't think our mission was the job for a patrol. If our Intelligence suspected that the VC were building an arsenal in that ravine, why didn't they simply blast it? We had the firepower even if we wasted it. The ways of the army brass are obscure but the ways of a patrol are not. The brass don't risk their lives. We do. We had our orders but we were not about to carry them out stupidly. We stayed put at the edge of the woods watching for some indication of enemy activity. We didn't wait long.

○

Four Vietnamese in peasant dress, apparently unarmed, seemed to appear from nowhere. They came from the north and were cutting across the paddy toward the ravine. Their course convinced Doll that they were VC and he wanted to open fire on them, but Thomas objected, reminding us that our orders were to observe and report without engaging the enemy unless necessary. In the seclusion of the trees, our vantage point was ideal and Doll was itching to fire on them. It was too good an opportunity to lose but he wasn't prepared to disobey the new patrol leader again, not with two witnesses who were unsympathetic. We watched the Vietnamese until they disappeared into the tangled foliage of the ravine. Thomas was uncertain of our next move and Doll supplied it. He said it was time to radio platoon headquarters and report our information and ask for military support to blast the ravine.

"We still don't know what the hell is in there," Thomas protested.

"We know there's four VC in there," Doll countered. "Tell them we saw eight."

"That's a fucking lie."

"Yeah it is. You ready to cross that paddy and find out how many there is?"

"They'll have my ass if there's nothing else in that ravine but four unarmed gooks."

"How they gonna know? Eight VC's an enemy force. Just try it and tell them we got a gook already and we lost the old man. It'll give us points."

"You bastard."

"Yeah," Doll admitted. "You gonna get on that radio or what?"

Thomas was out of ideas. He radioed the platoon command and got the commander, Lieutenant Caldron, to whom he recited the events of the patrol. He did a thorough job, reporting the killing of the sniper and the death of Sergeant Stone. No mention was made of the killing of the boy. It was my first awareness that Thomas and Doll both intended to cover it up as if it had not happened.

With the map before him, Thomas gave the grid coordinates of the minefield and the location where the VC had entered the ravine. Lieutenant Caldron was impressed, and he readily agreed when Thomas hesitantly suggested artillery to hit that point of the ravine. He said he would dispatch gunships with rockets and machine guns to rake the entire area. He ordered the patrol to observe the attack from our position in the tree line and stay on the radio to guide the gunships to the target. If the situation warranted it, he would order additional troopers in the vicinity to the area. He told Thomas to sit tight with his patrol and maintain contact. Thomas was extraordinarily pleased with the lieutenant's response and took the entire credit for it to the chagrin of Doll, who nevertheless was ready to make concessions providing Thomas did.

We sat on the ground at the edge of the tree line, overlooking the paddy and waited for the gunships. We were relaxed until Doll popped out with his question.

"You still going to put me on report when we get back?" he asked Thomas.

Propped against a tree trunk, Thomas smiled tightly. "I'll think about it."

"Why don't you just forget it? You know I was right."

Thomas's body arched. "I know you let me down out there and I nearly got blasted by that gook. Man, I prayed you'd open up—but nothing, nothing." His accusation included all of us. "I can't forget that."

"We didn't know what was out there," Doll protested.

"Motherfucker! You didn't know what was in that bramble neither when you sprayed it—buffalo killer."

"I thought it was Charlie."

"And who the fuck did you think was shooting at me, huh?"

"We couldn't see nothing."

"Shit. You didn't have to see nothing. You know an AK when you hear it. But it wasn't your ass."

"Come on, Thomas. You ain't holding that against me? They was in on it, too."

"Yeah, but your ass was supposed to be out there getting that map. And if that gook had pinned you down I'da stuck my neck out. I did it for the old man and he was dead."

"You needed the map."

"*We* needed the map, bright boy. That map's bringing them gunships in here, ain't it? While you're cooling your ass in comfort and safety."

"That was my idea."

"Fuck you, Doll. Don't rile me. You gonna get all the points coming to you."

Doll clenched his teeth to keep silent. I thought Thomas had provoked him too much. Not that I blamed

Thomas. Doll had it coming. We did, too. But Doll was a vindictive bastard. I hoped he wouldn't act on it. I was afraid of him.

○

In a few minutes three gunships arrived in the area. They circled high over the paddy to get their bearings before making their strike. Thomas got on the radio to them and gave our location at the tree line. He pinpointed the spot where the VC had entered the ravine and the gunships went into action. They wheeled off behind us and then came in low at treetop level. The roar of their motors was soothing. We were no longer alone. They swept across the paddy field directly on target. Flying abreast, they fired their rockets fifty meters into the ravine from its edge. At the same time, the door gunners poured machine-gun fire across the ravine. Their firepower was deafening, and I watched with fascination as they reached the end of their run and rose up sharply to clear the hills. The ravine swallowed up their rocket fire and all was still again as the gunships circled back over the woods. There was no sign of the enemy. There had been no ground fire from the ravine or the hills.

"We fucked up again," Thomas said worriedly to Doll. Doll said nothing.

The gunships roared back for a second strike, this time bearing to the right. They repeated the same flat out attack. The rockets scored. A huge explosion erupted in a ball of fire and debris from the ravine. With their machine guns rattling, the gunships started their climb.

"An ammunition dump!" Doll said gleefully and he clapped Thomas on the back. "Ain't it beautiful?"

"Beautiful, man."

We watched the gunships shudder up in their climb. It is the moment when a chopper hangs between its forward flight and its upward lift. The enemy knows that moment and waits for it. This time Charlie was ready. Automatic gunfire opened up from the hill on a line with the choppers. The two outside gunships peeled apart. The

49

center one was turning to the left when it burst into flame. Its torn parts plunged into the green hillside, leaving no trace of its violent death. The suddenness of its disappearance stunned us all. Except Doll. He was too excited by the action and our having located the enemy. He pressed Thomas to report the news to headquarters and ask for ground artillery support and more gunships. Thomas responded, relieved to have his thinking done for him. His vivid description of the ground explosion in the ravine elated Lieutenant Caldron. The loss of the gunship was accepted routinely. The lieutenant asked again for the coordinates of the ravine and informed Thomas that ground artillery would zero in. Also, Thomas was told that two squads operating in the vicinity would be dispatched to the paddy field to move on the ravine with his patrol. That last piece of information shook me. Doll detected my concern and struck at it.

"You ain't fired your fucking rifle all day, kid. Yeah. I noticed. But now you're running out of excuses. Old Charlie's waiting in that ravine for you and he don't have no sympathy for scared punks. And neither do I."

"Lay off the kid, Doll," Blondy said. "It's his first patrol. Give him a chance."

"The motherfucker had two chances already. He never fired at the gook in the tree or at the buffalo."

"I didn't fire at the buffalo, neither. Some of us ain't trigger-happy."

"You better be trigger-ready when we cross that paddy unless you want to be KIA."

"From Charlie or you?"

Doll didn't answer but he met Blondy's accusing gaze without flinching. They understood each other and I understood them. Their hostility sent a shiver up my back.

○

In the next hour the action increased considerably and we were in the thick of it with no time for personal distractions. The two gunships were joined by three more and they concentrated their attack on the ravine where the ammunition dump had blown up. In addition, spotter planes were on the scene to direct the fire of the ground artillery. We watched the build-up of the attack until the two squads arrived on our left flank. Then we joined with them to cross the paddy while the gunships dived on the enemy emplacements in the hills and our artillery raked the ravine. It was an all-out effort. Luckily, the VC were too busy firing at the gunships to shell our advance through the paddy. Aside from a couple of mortar rounds that churned up the earth, we crossed to the edge of the ravine without incident. Our orders now were to penetrate the ravine and engage the enemy at close quarters. It was the moment I had dreaded most of all. For some reason I didn't understand at the time, I was less fearful of losing my own life than taking the life of the enemy. I thought about Blondy's remark that the killing would "come by itself." I didn't think so, nor did Doll. He kept an eye on me, waiting for me to blunder.

Our ground artillery ceased firing before we got in close. In my two days at camp I had heard stories of men being killed by their own ground support, stories that the survivors had related with extreme caution because the brass didn't want them to leak out. It was bad for morale situation, radio communication was good and Lieutenant Caldron did a careful job of coordinating the action of all and very bad for the army's image back home. In our the elements in the attack.

In a final strike before pulling out, the gunships rocketed a point halfway up the ravine. They hit more than trees and dirt. Whatever it was, it exploded and burned, sending up bright orange swirls of flame. It was an encouraging sight as we plunged into the thick vines of the ravine.

It was tough going. The tangle of undergrowth was so dense that we couldn't see each other five meters apart. My patrol stayed together with the two squads on our flanks. We moved like an arrow in slow motion with Doll leading, followed by Thomas and Blondy and me side by side behind. All around us troopers swore aloud as their weapons or clothing were caught on the prickly vines. The heat was brutal and our efforts to cut through the tangle made it unbearable. But the size of our numbers and the activity in the air was comforting. It made me feel safe even if I wasn't.

Except for our own sounds, it was quiet in the tangle—too quiet. We must have gone about forty meters, fifty at the most, when the quiet ended in a full-scale firefight. Automatic gunfire hit us from both sides and in front. In that jungle I couldn't see where it came from but rounds sang overhead and through the brush. Many found their mark as GI's screamed with pain and disappeared into the undergrowth. I was too scared to think about anything but protecting myself. Only later did I think it amazing that so many of the enemy could be entrenched in that ravine after it had been so thoroughly pummeled by rockets and ground fire. Charlie's ability to survive was the most astounding fact I learned from that year of war.

All around me, guns blazed in a steady tattoo at the unseen enemy. Only my M-16 was silent. I held my fire because Blondy and other troopers were now ahead of me and I was deathly afraid of hitting them. The firing went on blindly, increasing the confusion in our ranks. Troopers barked orders contradicting one another. As a result, none were obeyed. Word spread that the leaders of both squads had been killed. That compounded the anarchy.

It was Doll who created order out of the chaos. He screamed at the top of his voice for everyone to hold his fire. His voice commanded authority and his message got through. We broke off firing. To our surprise, the enemy did too. The silence was eerie. We dug in and waited, listening hard for any sound that would tell us where the VC were. All was quiet.

Doll scrambled around in the underbrush and found out that both squads had lost their radio operators. Their radios had been knocked out with them. We had the only operable radio. Thomas raised platoon headquarters and Doll did the talking. He reported the grids of our position and our encounter with the enemy force. He told Lieutenant Caldron we were outnumbered and pinned down. I had to admire his forcefulness in handling the lieutenant's queries:

"How many VC are there?"

"A helluva lot more than us, lieutenant."

"But we pasted the hell out of them before you went in."

"Yeah, but they're still here."

"What about the other two squads?"

"They're here, bleeding."

"Where's their CO's? Why don't they call in?"

"They're dead. The RTO's got hit too and their radios are out."

"How many dead and wounded?"

"Enough. You want a fucking count?"

"Take it easy, corporal."

"Yes sir, lieutenant."

"What do you need?"

"More firepower. The gunships hit something big before we moved in. The gooks are sitting on what's left."

"Can't you take it?"

"Not with this bunch."

"Where's Corporal Thomas?"

"He's right here holding the fucking radio—sir."

"He should be making the report."

"I got the info. It saves time giving it directly."

"Right. You're on the scene. What do you think, corporal? We can give you artillery fire but it sounds pretty tight."

"It is. Charlie's no more'n forty meters away. It don't give us much breathing space."

"We don't want to increase our own casualties."

"Yes sir. We don't want to be increased."

"Then get the hell out of there. Pull back to the paddy. I'll send in Cobras."

"Give us ten minutes to get out the dead and wounded."

"Right. Ten minutes. Keep Thomas alive. He's got the only working radio."

"Yes sir. Thank you, sir."

53

"Ten minutes. Get moving and stay on the horn."

We retreated back toward the paddy, taking our dead and wounded with us. Charlie smelled our pull back and opened fire. We left a handful of troopers to cover our rear. Our flanks were unprotected but we took no fire from them. The density of the jungle worked in our favor. The VC didn't move out of their position. Whatever they had stockpiled in that ravine, they intended to protect it.

By the time we slashed our way through the vines back to the rim of the ravine, two medical evacuation choppers were coming in across the paddy. From the hills the enemy started dropping mortar rounds into the valley around us. They exploded the wet earth into geysers of mud. We kept down in the screen of the foliage to wait for the choppers to set down. The loading had to be done rapidly. The choppers wouldn't land for more than a few seconds.

During the entire operation, Doll directed the activity and oversaw the evacuation. He had assumed leadership and no one questioned it. Without their CO's, the two squads were relieved to have someone take charge. Even Thomas went along. The confusion in the woods had bordered on panic and Doll's role in getting us out gave him quick status.

With the mortar barrage pockmarking the paddy, the choppers stayed off and called for suppressive fire. Doll got on the horn to them and relayed our condition. We had four dead and five wounded. Within minutes, our ground artillery had laid down a steady barrage of fire on the hills to allow the choppers to get in. It went smooth as clockwork. The choppers whirled in. Before their skids touched down, the medics jumped out with stretchers and hurried to us. The dead were loaded first without much care. Two of the wounded, seriously hurt, were carried out on stretchers. The medics treated them gingerly. The other three wounded managed to scramble out under their own power. The pilots kept their rotors churning and motioned for them to hurry. In less than a minute the whole evacuation was completed and the choppers lifted off in a roar of power and were gone, scooting across the paddy and rising swiftly above the tree line. We were relieved to have that burden off our weary backs. During the operation we didn't take a single mortar round, so heavy was the suppressive fire of our artillery.

Once the choppers were out, Doll radioed the results and our position to Lieutenant Caldron and was informed that the heavily armed Cobras were on their way.

○

The firefight lasted all afternoon. The diving Cobras concentrated their firepower on the section of the ravine where we had encountered the enemy while our artillery poured a steady stream of shells into the hills. The coordinated attack reduced the enemy fire from the hills so the Cobras could strike with greater precision at the ravine. From time to time their rockets touched off explosions under the carpet of green jungle where the VC were entrenched. The answering fire of small arms was sporadic and ineffective and after a while it stopped altogether, allowing the Cobras to skim over the treetops and pulverize the ground below. Each fresh explosion shook the earth and the tremors reached us two hundred meters away at the edge of the paddy.

Throughout the attack, Doll stayed on the radio guiding the gunships and spotting for the artillery. He relayed the effectiveness of the attack to platoon headquarters. Lieutenant Caldron was exhilarated by the news and commended Doll on the patrol's success in pinpointing the enemy stronghold. Doll was pleased. It was a busy and satisfying afternoon for him. He won the admiration of the troopers for his efficiency in directing the fight and managing to keep them out of it. We were all greatly relieved to hole up at the edge of the ravine and let the fighting be done for us.

With the approach of darkness, our artillery stopped firing and the Cobras made a last strike before breaking off for the night. As they returned to base, the diminishing sound of their rotors underlined the growing silence around us. One minute there had been the strangely comforting screams of the exploding shells and the next they were gone, leaving us with a silence that was ominous. It was the beginning of my first night in the field with the enemy, if he was still there, only two hundred meters away. I prayed he would take the night off.

Our orders were to stay put in our positions for the night and then move back into the ravine in the morning to reconnoiter the results of the Cobras' attack. We settled in, establishing a tight defensive night watch. I lay down in the undergrowth with my back touching the back of Blondy so that the movements of one would arouse the other. It was uncomfortable but it reassured us that one would not be killed without waking the other. Still, I did not sleep a wink that night in Vietnam. My mind whirled with the events of my first day of combat. I had been ill-prepared for them. It is one thing to be told that every Vietnamese is a potential enemy and must be destroyed, and quite another to carry it out. My thoughts returned repeatedly to the killing of the boy. Was I the only one in the patrol disturbed by it? Was his death simply another casualty of the war like the deaths of Sergeant Stone and the sniper and the water buffalo? Was there no difference? I could not accept killing without purpose. It made all life in this war, including my own, meaningless. I was obsessed by the image of the boy on the riverbank. If I didn't report the circumstances of his death, would it ever come out? I was determined that it must. If I kept silent, I would be a party to the atrocity. My conscience rebelled. Yet I was afraid to speak out alone. I wanted someone in the patrol to corroborate the facts. But who? I dismissed Doll and Thomas. Clearly, Doll didn't give a damn about any life but his own. And Thomas was an unlikely choice to buck the system, particularly in a situation that meant condemning the act of his patrol leader and a dead man to boot. That left only Blondy. He had shown no outward concern at the killing of the boy but I had to know how he felt about it. He was my only hope of support for my decision.

O

We were lying back to back in the undergrowth. It was hours after it had gotten dark. We had eaten our cold rations and afterwards Blondy had cursed because he couldn't smoke a joint. He wanted one badly. So did I. But it was too dangerous to show a light. Everyone was holed up for the night except the troopers on watch. Our security was in their hands. I lay awake listening to the night sounds of the jungle, straining to hear any man-made noise beyond our perimeter. After a while my tension lessened. I could hear Blondy's uneven breathing and knew he wasn't asleep. I wondered if the same thoughts were keeping him awake. I shifted on my back and nudged him. He rolled to face me. We talked in a whisper.

"It's been some day," I said.

"Yeah. But it's one day less. That's what counts."

"Is it always like this?"

"I seen a lot worse but you got a good taste for your first day."

"What do you mean—worse?"

"I mean more killing."

"And throat-cutting?"

"Forget about that kid. That was nothing."

"I can't forget about it."

"What about the old man? Don't that bother you?"

"Sure. But he didn't have to kill the boy. There was no reason."

"He couldn't wait for no reason. The kid might have got us all killed. You think of that?"

"How? He told us the VC were across the river. He was too scared to go with us."

"So what?"

"So he wasn't the enemy. He was just a kid out fishing for food."

57

"Shit. You'da let him go, huh? So he could hustle his ass back to that village and report our position. We'da been ambushed inside ten minutes."

"You really believe that kid was a VC?"

"He's dead and every dead gook is a VC."

"You sound like Doll. I thought you were different."

"Fuck you, Glass. What do you know? Doll's a butcher. There's a lot of butchers out here but I ain't one of them. I never butchered nobody in two hundred and thirty-three days. Thirty-four. I never even sliced off an ear and that's standard operating procedure. And I didn't slice that kid's throat but I ain't sitting judgment on it. That ain't why I'm here."

"Yeah, you're nothing like Doll," I said apologetically. "But don't you see that killing a civilian kid is different than cutting off the ear of a dead soldier?"

"I only know what I can do and can't do. I live with everything else that happens here. And you better learn that fast if you want to make it."

I stuck to my decision. "When we get back I'm going to report exactly what happened to that kid. Somebody's got to talk for him."

"He's dead and the old man's dead. What does it matter now?"

"I'm not dead. It matters to me."

"You're out of your fucking mind. You're all worked up because this is your first patrol. Believe me, I know what you're feeling. I been through it. But you get used to it. You'll forget all about that kid in a couple of days. You'll forget a lot worse than today before you're through here."

"You don't understand. I don't want to forget."

"You let everything get to you and you'll end up in the psycho ward."

I said nothing. The gap between us was too wide. But Blondy didn't let it drop. He was concerned for me and I appreciated that.

"Listen to me, Glass. When we get back, you let Doll and Thomas do the talking, you hear? Whatever they say is the way it is. You open your mouth to the lieutenant and you'll be in big trouble. Doll's a mean bastard. I know his kind. And he don't like you already. He can make it real bad for you. Real bad, you understand?"

"What can he do?"

"He can make you a friendly casualty. Put a bullet in you, that's what. Don't mess with him. And you better fire your fucking rifle at something before we hit camp. It's all right to be scared but not for too long. You hear?"

"I hear. Thanks."

Blondy rolled onto his side and I pressed my back up against his for the rest of the night. He had disappointed me but I was glad he wasn't a butcher.

○

Shortly after dawn we started to move back into the ravine. I welcomed the first light filtering through the trees. It calmed me. As we proceeded cautiously through the tangle, I was again struck by the absurdity of the situation. The jungle sounds were so pleasant it was difficult to believe that an unseen enemy was out there waiting to kill us. My instinct was to bolt from that ravine and run from that valley. I'd had more than enough of butchery and death. But I plodded forward, obeying the commands, my rifle at the ready. Only my light-headedness, generated by the joint Blondy had given me at daybreak, kept me as together as I was. Grass was my secret strength, my only comfort in that ravine.

A hundred meters farther into the jungle we saw the first signs of the Cobras' attack. Trees were uprooted in a tangle of scarred vines and the thick undergrowth was pitted with craters. A small body in black pajamas, not much larger than the boy on the riverbank, lay sprawled in one of the craters. A direct hit had sheared off his arms. His bare feet were clotted with blood but his head was unmarked, crumpled into his shoulder, and his rifle was still strapped to his body.

Doll was the first to reach him. Scrambling into the

crater, he cut off one of the dead man's ears and thrust it into his rucksack with the amputated finger. Right with him, Thomas retrieved the rifle and slung it over his shoulder. They made an efficient team of scavengers, each satisfied with his own take. Other troopers joined them and fleeced the remains—a cartridge belt, the other ear, the nose, the toes. So it went. The mutilated corpse gave up its parts for souvenirs and the enemy body count soared.

We pushed on. The jungle was burned brown from the fire bombs. It was hot and steamy and silent except for the chirping of the birds. Somehow, they had survived the devastating attack. And somehow, so had the enemy. There were no more bodies to pluck.

But there was much evidence that the enemy had been there. Supplies were strewn everywhere. Shredded bags of rice lay on the ground and hung from the vines and branches; twisted pieces of machine-gun barrels, gun mounts and ammunition drums littered an area of forty meters. Scurrying through the debris, the troopers started collecting souvenirs. Suddenly, a grenade popped in the bushes and a trooper screamed. We dropped to the ground as the wounded trooper stumbled into the clearing. Half his face had been blown off, leaving a gaping hole of pulp and blood. He was clutching the barrel of a machine gun as he wobbled toward us, staring dazedly with his remaining eye. Before anyone could get to him, he pitched forward on his face and lay still.

A second grenade went off on our right. A second trooper appeared out of the bushes, his left hand shattered at the wrist and dripping blood. "Everything's booby-trapped," he muttered.

Doll was on his feet shouting that nothing was to be touched. Charlie had concealed grenades under most of his equipment. With the pins half-pulled, they exploded with the slightest jarring. The souvenir hunters had been psyched out. It cost one dead and one wounded and it made Doll furious. He couldn't understand how Charlie had survived the Cobra attack and then carefully planted the grenades. He called them scum, animals, inhuman, and swore that we'd slaughter them before the day was out.

The wounded man was sent back to the paddy with a trooper to wait for a chopper and the dead man was left untouched to be carried out later. With Doll leading, we pressed deeper into the ravine, picking our way slowly, cautiously, fearful of grenades and mines. There was no sign of the retreating enemy. He was gone with his wounded and dead. It was apparent that while we had languished in the night waiting for dawn, the VC had been busy mining their leavings for our pickings. Would their escape route be our deathtrap? If the thought occurred to Doll, he dismissed it. He was convinced that Charlie had been badly mauled and was limping away under the burden of his losses. He was bent on catching him before he reached the safety of the hills. Though we didn't share his conviction, there was nothing to do but grumble and follow him. No one was in a position to question his leadership except Thomas, and he seemed content to let Doll run things.

We hacked our way up the rise of the ravine for another hundred meters. The tangle was so dense over our heads that we couldn't see the sky, but the heat was relentless and the air wet and stifling. With each step, we panted heavily and breathed through our mouths. Gnats and flies swarmed around our faces, attracted by the smell of sweat. It took all our energy to tear our way through the web of vines and branches, and the deeper we penetrated the more dense was the vegetation. After a while the troopers began to gripe and curse more loudly about everything they could think of—the jungle, the heat, the stupid enemy that picked this craphole to fight in and the stupid command that ordered them here. Finally, they focused their wrath on the man leading them.

"Where the fuck is that fucking corporal taking us?"

"We got no orders to cut through this shit."

"What the hell is that motherfucker looking for?"

"A field promotion, dumb ass!"

And on and on.

Doll heard some of the remarks but he ignored them.

61

What the troopers thought of him didn't bother him. He was in command and he was concerned only with tracking the enemy and killing him. Like a man possessed, he pushed on, thrashing through the jungle. Stumbling, cursing, we pursued him another ten meters and another. The sweltering heat and the clawing, prickly vines sapped our strength and aggravated our nerves.

Another ten meters farther and the ground rose up sharply. We had crossed the ravine and reached the foot of the hills. Doll called a halt to consider the situation. Instead of being relieved that the ravine was cleared of the enemy, he was openly disappointed in not having made contact. He ranted about the little gook bastards having hit us and run. The weary troopers didn't share his feelings. They flopped in the grass and lit joints. The sweet smell irritated Doll and he regarded them with contempt. But he said nothing.

Studying the rise of the hills, he said loudly to Thomas, "The fuckers are in there. I know it. They're dragging their dead. How far could they get?"

"I don't know. But we ain't got the muscle to go up there. That's VC territory. They been sitting on it for years. It ain't our job to clean them out."

"Yeah, man," a trooper called out.

"It's our job to find Charlie and kill him," Doll snapped.

Where had I heard that before? The language of leadership in the mouth of a butcher.

"We lost four dead and five wounded yesterday and two more men this morning," Doll went on. "And all we got to show for it is one dead gook back there."

"It ain't a numbers game," Blondy said. "We cleared the ravine. That's more'n we came for."

"We cleared shit. The gunships did it."

"The gunships are us. It's the same thing."

"I say we go up there after them."

"We ain't supposed to be this far," Blondy protested. "They hold the hills and we're sitting down here in this fucking tangle like chickens in a henhouse. We're lucky they ain't mortaring us right now."

"They don't know we're here yet. I tell you them gooks are sweating up them hills right now. We can catch them."

"The lieutenant told us to reconnoiter the ravine. He didn't say nothing about chasing Charlie into them hills."

"Blondy's right," Thomas said. "We got no orders."

"In the field you react to the situation. You know that, Thomas."

Thomas met Doll's intent gaze. I watched the sweat stream down his face and dribble from his broad, black nose onto his fat lips as they curled into a hard smile. "Yeah," he said, "and my personal reaction is to get the lieutenant on the horn and tell *him* the situation. He's getting decision pay. You ain't. I ain't."

Doll looked flustered. He hadn't expected opposition from Thomas but he held his ground. It was showdown time. "You questioning my decision, Thomas? I'm leading this outfit now, remember?"

"I remember everything, baby. Everything." Thomas tapped the side of his head.

Doll pressed his view. "I say we push up the hill."

Thomas responded by clicking on the radio. "Tell it to the lieutenant. Let's hear what he says."

"Shut that fucking thing off!" Doll reached out and flipped off the switch. "We don't need the lieutenant. He ain't here. We are."

"Cool it, man. We ain't going up no fucking hill on your say-so. Don't you dig? I ain't putting my black ass on the line for you, baby. Shit, what you humping for—sergeant stripes?"

"You're the fucking number two man, Thomas, just like with the old man."

"Yeah, only you ain't the old man."

All around us, the troopers grunted approval of Thomas's position. Doll saw his command crumbling in the faces of the men. "Get the lieutenant," he said to Thomas. "I'll report the morning's operation."

"Yazzuh," Thomas said.

Nobody laughed.

Thomas opened radio contact and Doll briefed the lieutenant on the morning's action. Lieutenant Caldron was enthusiastic about the news that the ravine had been cleared and he again commended Doll and the men for their part in the operation, saying he would report the results to company headquarters. Doll seized the moment to request permission to pursue the enemy into the hills, stressing his view that Charlie was disabled and on the run and we could increase his casualties. To my surprise and relief, Lieutenant Caldron displayed a hard-headed understanding of the situation.

"What's your position now?" the lieutenant asked.

"We're on the edge of the ravine at the base of the hills."

"You pushed in far enough. You don't have the men to push up those hills."

"But Charlie's hurting bad, lieutenant. If we catch him on the slopes we can slaughter him."

"And you might get slaughtered. He's got plenty of firepower up top to pour down on you."

"He wouldn't fire into his own positions."

"Can you see Charlie on the slopes?"

"No sir. It's too dense. But he's in there. I know it."

"You pull back, corporal, before he clears the slopes and starts raking your position."

"Yes sir. But I still say—"

"Get your men out of there. You did your job. When command decides to take the hills, we'll let you know."

"Yes sir."

"Call in when you get back to the paddy and we'll hit the slopes with artillery. If Charlie's still in there, we'll do the job for you."

"By that time he'll be on top, lieutenant."

"Goddammit, stop bucking me, corporal. I'm ordering you to pull out right now. I don't want to lose any more men. Command's satisfied with this operation. I don't want you lousing it up now."

"Yes sir."

"Now hustle your ass."

Several troopers started moving back through the ravine without waiting for the order from Doll. Their action infuriated him and he ordered them to halt until he and Thomas had pushed ahead of them to lead the way. He was plainly disgusted with the lieutenant's decision, bitching loudly to Thomas that it was no goddamn way to fight a war. You didn't hit the enemy and then back off just when you had him on the ropes. Gunships and artillery were necessary to knock out installations and soften resistance but it took combat troops to take enemy ground and hold it. If you didn't do that then what the hell was all the goddamn fighting for? "Charlie'll be right back in this fucking ravine tomorrow and we'll be back here clearing it again."

"Yeah," Thomas said indifferently. "That's the way it is."

"But it don't have to be that way. We got the ravine. We ought to hold it and then take them hills."

"Who's we?"

"The United States Army. Us."

"I ain't the United States Army. I'm just Corporal Jefferson Thomas putting in his time. How come you're so fired up? You're just a fucking corporal like me, man. Leave the strategy to the brass. It's their war. Don't you know that yet?"

"It's your war as long as you're here."

"My war is staying alive. I fight that every fucking day and the United States Army don't help me."

○

Going out was easier than going in. Our morale was better and we didn't have to worry about mines as long as we stayed on the trail we had already used. Even Doll's spirits rose. The lieutenant's satisfaction with the mission had begun to register in his angry head. His obsession to slaughter Charlie evaporated and he began to chatter excitedly about the success of the operation and the likelihood that we'd all get commendations and maybe promotions. Why not?

The sudden change in Doll's mood made me nervous.

I couldn't figure him out unless he was plain crazy. In the day and a half I'd known him he had shown only one consistency. He hated Charlie. I'd seen the pleasure in his face when he sawed off the finger of the dead sniper and again when he cut the ear of the VC in the ravine. I thought about his trophies. In a year he could amass quite a collection. Would he decorate his house with them? I pictured a wall of ears and another of fingers and I heard his appropriate commentary for each: "I got this finger off a dead gook in a tree who had us pinned down in the Central Highlands. And this ear belonged to a little gink we found in a crater with his arms sheared off by rocket fire. That was some day. You should have been there. We cleaned out a whole ravine—supplies, ammunition. It cost us five, six men, but it was worth it. We had those gooks on the run until the stupid brass made us pull back. We could of taken them hills. We had them on the ropes."

My fantasy about Corporal Doll ended abruptly. We had reached the clearing where we'd left the dead GI. On orders from Doll two troopers started to lift the body, when the mine underneath it blew up in their faces and tore the dead man from their grasp. The force of the explosion threw them several feet. They landed on the ground, clutching their faces. The booby-trapped corpse lay face up between them, a fresh, gaping hole in the chest. Wheeling around in the clearing, Doll searched the tangle for the enemy. Though everything was still, he held his rifle at waist level and raked the bushes in quick crackling bursts until his clip was empty. Nervously, the troopers opened fire in the same direction. Bullets snapped and whined through the underbrush. Beside me, Blondy blazed away and I started firing my rifle for the first time. I was so tensed up I failed to let up on the trigger and the gun jumped in my grip until I had emptied the magazine. My hands shook as I tried to reload. The indiscriminate firing went on for several minutes until Doll's voice rose above the din: "Hold your fire!"

It was almost a minute before the troopers realized

they weren't in a firefight, that Doll's outrage had provoked them to fire senselessly into the harmless jungle.

"What the fuck you doing?" Thomas shouted at Doll. "There ain't nobody out there."

"Charlie's out there," Doll rasped and he rammed a fresh clip into his rifle. "He mined that fucking corpse and got two more men." His gaze went to the wounded troopers as if he suddenly remembered their existence. "Get them on their feet."

A trooper, administering first aid, said, "They're bleeding pretty bad."

"Yeah, get them up."

"Let's get the hell out of here," Thomas said.

Doll glowered at him. "You get headquarters and tell them to send in a chopper for the wounded. We'll get to the paddy in ten minutes. Ten minutes, you hear? And then I want to blast this fucking ravine off the map. Tell them!"

Two troopers started to lift the body of the dead man when Doll screamed at them: "Leave him. Take his fucking dog tags and ammo belt. That's all we need."

○

We were less than a hundred meters from the paddy, still wrestling our way through the undergrowth, when we heard the whirring rotors of the evacuation chopper in the distance. It was a soothing sound. I was wishing that I'd be evacuated with the wounded when the first mortar round whooshed in on our right. Another round came in directly ahead of us and then a third off to our left. We flopped in our tracks. The wounded screamed as they were dropped by the men carrying them. From the hills above and behind us came the steady popping of the mortars and then, seconds later, the explosions, cracking the trees and throwing up clumps of earth. We were boxed in. Charlie had our position and was laying down a pattern of shells. Above the explosion I could hear Thomas on the radio calling frantically for suppressive fire. A shell whistled in and exploded in our midst. Two troopers hurtled through the air

67

above me and crashed into the bramble. From behind a trooper shouted, "Jesus Christ! Let's get the hell out of here!" He scrambled past us into the undergrowth toward the paddy.

Doll yelled at him to stay down but the trooper paid no attention and disappeared into the bushes. Within seconds, troopers were on their feet scurrying after him, and the panic was on.

At first, Doll was furious, bellowing at them to stay put until we got artillery support, but he quickly realized it was hopeless. With the shells exploding in a steady tattoo, no one was listening to him. At that moment he was a leader without troops. Only Thomas, Blondy and I remained at his side. Doll stared in disbelief at the fleeing troopers. "Yellow fuckers!" he raged. "I'll have you all court-martialed!"

A shell burst five meters away, pouring dirt down on us. Blondy jumped to his feet. "It's better to get it moving than waiting for it," he said to Doll.

"You stay here!" Doll shrieked at him. But Blondy was gone, darting off after the others.

Instantly, Doll raised his rifle and aimed it at the bushes where Blondy had disappeared. Beside him, Thomas reached out and firmly grasped the gun barrel and held it. Doll tried to jerk it from his grasp.

"Get yourself together, corporal," Thomas said. "You don't want to do that, man."

Doll's red face blanched under Thomas's cold gaze. "You got two witnesses, Doll. We don't want you to be worrying about us, do we?"

Doll's eyes narrowed. "Let go of the rifle."

"Sure, man." Thomas released his grip. "Now let's get our ass out of here and join the troops." He stood up in a crouch behind Doll. I got up beside him. "You're the number one man," he said flatly. "I'll follow you."

Without a word, Doll sprang forward into the tangle and we followed him.

○

Bearing our wounded, we pushed and clawed and battered our way through the undergrowth, heedless of the shells bursting on all sides, and somehow we managed to reach the paddy without taking any more casualties. High overhead, the evacuation chopper circled beyond the range of the VC guns, now mortaring the paddy. We flattened ourselves on the ground in the high grass and waited for the guns to let up. There was nothing else to do except pray and curse, and the men did both in frustration and anger at the helplessness of our situation.

To a man, the troopers' anger was directed openly at Doll for having led them to the end of the ravine and back into the trap we were now in. His moody, erratic leadership had botched the mission for them and wasted lives. Their bitterness overcame the military discipline that had been drilled into them. There were threats about "getting" Doll if the bombardment didn't let up. Everyone's nerves were raw. I felt the troopers were at the point of rebellion. It frightened me. Doll must have sensed it, too. He acted desperately to regain his command and save his skin. He got on the radio to platoon headquarters and screamed at the lieutenant for suppressive fire.

"It's been ordered!" Lieutenant Caldron barked.

"Then where the hell is it? The gooks are blasting the shit out of us. We got wounded to get out and the chopper can't get in."

"Don't panic, corporal. It's coming now."

"It better or we'll all be dead in the next five minutes."

"Keep your head, corporal. You're responsible for the safety of your men."

"Yeah, yeah."

"After the chopper is out, get your men across the paddy. We'll keep the hills busy. I want your outfit back here by nightfall. You understand?"

69

"Yes sir."

"Good. You should be getting our support fire right now."

Doll released a chestful of breath. "Shut that fucking radio," he said to Thomas. Then he stood up in the grass and scanned the sky.

In the distance we heard the dull thumping of our artillery and then the shells started screaming over and exploding in the hills. Abruptly, the mortaring fell off.

"The chopper's coming in," Doll shouted. "Soon as it's loaded we'll head for the tree line and regroup there. We're heading back to camp."

There were grunts of relief from the troopers. For the moment, the threats against Doll's life were forgotten.

○

After the chopper took out the wounded, we made quick time across the paddy. It was easier going in the open and we were buoyed up to be on our way out. A couple of mortar rounds burst harmlessly off to our right. They were the last shells from the VC, who were now getting the full brunt of our artillery.

At the tree line, we flopped down to rest and eat and watch the show in the hills. The change in circumstances elated the troopers. Like spectators at a game, they responded gleefully at the sight of the explosions tearing up the VC terrain.

"The fuckers are eating it now," one of them cackled. "Kill them! Wipe them out!"

I looked around at their watchful faces, grinning now, all the fear and anguish I had seen in the ravine gone. Their reaction was natural after what we'd been through. I envied the simplicity of their response. I didn't share it. Looking across at those hills, I felt no hatred for the men in them. Those were their hills, their valley, their country. Why were we here trying to take it away from them?

In basic training the army hadn't dealt with motive. At eighteen, protected by the decency of my orphanage world, I knew little of the indecency of the world outside, a world in which men readily killed men to avoid being killed. Oh,

70

since those days of my first patrol, I have learned something of the ways of nations and men and the politics that motivate them. But then, in that forest, looking across that paddy at the violence in the hills, I saw life and death with a simple clarity that sufficed for me. I had reason to despise the brutality and the reckless ambition of a Corporal Doll, and to understand the troopers' hatred for an enemy that took their lives and for a leader that exploited them. But I had an awareness of my own innocence that resisted the corruption around me. It was at that moment, I think, that I realized why I had been reluctant to fire my rifle. I didn't want to take a life without knowing why. And it was then that I resolved not to kill any Vietnamese except to save my own life.

○

Lying under the trees, smoking a joint Blondy had given me and watching the shelling in the hills, I played the numbers game, tabulating a debit and credit sheet of the mission.

Our losses: Sergeant Stone, dead; one gunship and crew, destroyed; four dead and five wounded, ambushed; one dead and one wounded from mortar fire. That made a total of six dead and ten wounded, plus the gunship crew.

Enemy losses: one boy, dead; one sniper, dead; one VC, dead—armless, earless, noseless, toeless—in the ravine. A total of three bodies.

The attack by the Cobras and our artillery may have accounted for additional enemy dead and wounded unknown to us but I took no solace from that.

I'd had my fill of death and I trembled as I puffed my way hungrily into the more peaceful world of birdsong and chattering monkeys in the trees. I was high on grass and it was all I had to go on with.

○

I don't remember the hour or more it took us to hike through the woods, except that we must have followed the same course back because we came across the dead water

71

buffalo and I wondered whose side it had died for. And I remembered, too, that Doll cautioned the men not to touch the animal for fear that it might be mined. But his warning was unnecessary. No one wanted a buffalo souvenir.

○

I was clearheaded by the time we returned to the river at the same place we had crossed it. The dead sniper, with his finger missing, wasn't in the tree, but we found the old man still in the bushes where we had dragged him—only his body was stripped naked and he had been decapitated. A head for a finger.

There was no point in calling in a chopper to take him out. He wasn't any good to anybody now. We left him there for the maggots to find out if his corpse was mined and we hurried back across the river, staying clear of the shoals.

○

Going through the high grass in single file, Doll led the way with Thomas three yards behind him and the rest of us spaced the same distance apart. The afternoon heat enveloped us in a steam bath. Sweat burned our eyes and streamed down our faces. Cut and smarting from the grasses whipping at our faces and arms, we stumbled forward oblivious of everything but our exhaustion and the throbbing pain in our limbs. From time to time, a trooper slipped and fell heavily and was pulled back on his feet by the weary man behind. Someone suggested halting to rest but Doll insisted that we had to push ahead to the base of the plateau. He was determined to carry out the lieutenant's orders and reach camp by nightfall. It was an unreasonable schedule. We couldn't make the climb up the trail in less than four hours and it would be dark before then. The troopers knew it and it revived their hostility against Doll. The line of men behind him began to rattle with hate. But if Doll heard it he paid it no mind, and maintained a steady, tormenting pace as if he were enjoying testing the patience and endurance of the men. He was perverse enough. Only Thomas marched in stoic silence. Despite the extra burden of the radio and the two VC rifles, he stayed doggedly on Doll's tail. After a while they pulled farther ahead of the rest of us but we made no effort to catch up. If they ran into trouble we'd know it soon enough, and if they didn't they'd just have to wait. Fuck them. It wasn't likely that Corporal Doll was going to keep his nightfall schedule without the rest of his shabby command. He figured on marching into camp at the head of his column.

From up ahead, Doll's voice crackled back at us: "Come on, move it along! We ain't got all day. It'll be dark pretty soon."

"Fuck you," a trooper rasped in a loud voice. Others echoed his sentiments in their own juicy language.

"What's that?" Doll yelled.

Blondy and I came upon him first. He was waiting for us, the sweat glistening on his red, freckled face. Thomas was beside him, holding his helmet and mopping his brow with his sleeve. I didn't know if Doll was so red-faced from the heat or the anger smoldering in him.

"You got something to say, Glass?" he barked.

"Nothing."

"You spit it out to my face, hear?"

"He didn't say nothing," Blondy said.

"Nobody asked you, you fuckup."

"Cool it, corporal," Thomas said calmly.

"You shut your ass! And don't call me corporal. You ain't the goddamn lieutenant."

Thomas looked surprised. "Easy, man. Don't look for no extra trouble. Ain't you had enough?"

"I'm still running this show and I don't want any more shit from this bunch." Doll looked past us at the troopers crowding up in the grass. "We got four, five more hours of marching ahead of us. That's the way it is and I don't want to hear no more bitching from no one. You're in big trouble already from back there. You understand? And we ain't clear of Charlie yet. The picnic ain't over. This whole

73

fucking valley's his stomping grounds. Now spread out again in line and keep it moving." He turned his back on us and stalked off through the grass. Thomas put his helmet back on and went after him.

"I could put a clean round right through his fucking thick skull," a trooper said. Someone else grunted. I looked away from their hostile faces and followed after Blondy.

The field of grass seemed endless and I was beginning to feel the mission was, too. It was hard to believe we'd been out less than two days. In my frightened head and aching body it felt more like a month.

○

The unexpected happens in Vietnam as quick as you can snap your fingers, quicker than you can fire your rifle. Five minutes and fifty meters after Doll's pep talk, automatic gunfire crackled off to our right and bullets hissed through the grass around us. We were on our bellies when a trooper shouted, "Charlie at three o'clock." It was after the fact, and anyway we couldn't see a thing through the thick grass. Doll bellowed at us to hold our fire.

We lay still and listened. The gunfire stopped and then opened up again and stopped. "Two VC, maybe three," Doll shouted.

They couldn't see us any more than we could see them; yet, outnumbered, they were attacking. I didn't understand why. The tactics of the enemy were obscure to me.

Doll passed the word that he was going to open fire and when he did he wanted every rifleman on his feet raking that field in a forty-five-degree arc. At the crack of his first burst, we were up and blasting away with the concentrated firepower of eighteen automatic rifles. It was all outgoing. Nothing came back at us. Down the line, troopers reloaded and kept up a continuous rattle of fire. I fired my clip into the air just over the tips of the grass. It satisfied me.

After three or four minutes, Doll called a halt to the firing. The field was again quiet and peaceful and alien.

We listened, waiting for the answering fire of the enemy. It didn't come. Doll was certain that we got the VC, and he scurried alone through the grass toward the spot where the gunfire had come from. It seemed foolish to me but by now nothing Doll did was surprising. Yet I was surprised when, after a moment, Thomas followed him. The rest of us stayed put and waited. They seemed to be gone a long time when we heard the single shot of a rifle and then a short burst of automatic gunfire and then silence again. Blondy looked worriedly at me. Down the line, troopers muttered uneasily, wondering what had happened. We waited, expecting more gunfire, but there was none. Finally we heard a rustling in the grass and the voice of Thomas calling out, "It's me. Don't shoot!"

Thomas loomed up in the grass, panting, and flopped down beside Blondy and me.

"What happened?" Blondy asked.

"One of the gooks got Doll. The gook was lying there, playing dead, and when Doll wasn't looking he fired his AK. I blasted him. There's two more dead out there with him."

"Jesus Christ!" Blondy said. "He was crazy to go out there. He was asking for it."

"Yeah."

"You were lucky."

"Yeah."

"What do we do now?"

Thomas sucked in his breath. "You and Glass get Doll. We'll carry him back to camp. We don't want to wait for a chopper. He's straight out about thirty meters. I'll raise the lieutenant and tell him the score."

Blondy nodded at me. "Let's go."

Nervously, I followed him through the high grass. We came on Doll lying on his belly. The whole back of his head was blown off. Next to him was the body of a VC, lying on his back. His dead eyes stared up at me. A clean bullet hole pierced his forehead just above the bridge of his nose. It looked like a third, glaring eye. He could have

75

been the older brother of the dead boy on the riverbank, the resemblance was so strong. Two more dead VC, shriveled in their black pajamas, lay side by side in the grass, their heads together as if they were asleep.

Without a word, we rolled Doll over on his back. I grasped the legs and Blondy took the arms and we carried him through the grass. He was much heavier than I had expected. With every step, his head bobbled loosely as if he were still alive. I half expected him to curse our clumsy handling of him.

When we got back to our position, Thomas reported that the lieutenant was furious at Doll for engaging the enemy. Our orders had been to avoid a firefight if possible. The lieutenant hadn't wanted any more losses.

"But we got three of them and only lost one," Blondy said. "You tell him that?"

"Yeah. I told him. It calmed him down."

I shook my head in disbelief.

"Something bothering you, Glass?" Thomas asked sharply.

"Nothing."

"Say it, man."

"It doesn't matter to Doll that the lieutenant's pissed, does it?"

"Doll was running things for himself, not for the good of the outfit. And he fucked up. You just remember that, Glass."

○

We carried Doll in two-man shifts. The troopers resented the added burden and were careless in their handling of the body. By the time we reached the base of the plateau, the dead man's face was a mass of bruises and cuts from the whipping blades of grass. No one gave a damn.

○

We rested at the bottom of the trail before starting the steep climb to the camp. It was getting dark but there was little danger ahead and we relaxed. I watched Thomas light up a joint and stare at the darkening sky. He fascinated me. I had underestimated him as a simple, accepting number two man. He now struck me as far more shrewd and complex than that. The old man was dead and Doll was dead, but Thomas had taken the same risks they had and he was alive. I respected him for that. He had calculated the odds and used them to work for him. I had some troubling thoughts about what may have happened to Doll back in the field but I forced them from my mind. It was not the time to raise them.

O

Our pace up the slope was slow, set by the teams struggling with the dead man. It took us four hours to reach the top of the plateau and another half-hour to make camp. When we marched into the perimeter, around nine-thirty, there was a good deal of activity. Troopers were preparing to go out on night ambush. Others stood around their tents, smoking and passing out advice to the departing men. No one paid us much attention until someone spotted the dead man and called out: "Who is it?"

"Corporal Doll," Blondy answered.

His reply raised interest. "Ain't he the guy who took over command in the ravine?"

"Yeah."

"Must a been rough. How many men you lose?"

"Ten, twelve."

Troopers gathered around us as we headed for the command tent of Lieutenant Caldron.

"How many gooks you get?" a trooper asked, noticing the AK's slung over Thomas's shoulder.

"Enough," Thomas grunted.

The trooper persisted. "How many?"

"Too many to count."

"Bullshit. Where's their rifles? You only got two."

"Fuck off," Thomas said.

"We cleared the VC out of that ravine," one of our troopers boasted.

"Yeah. We heard all about it."

77

"The lieutenant was dancing a jig this morning. You guys are in for a commendation."

"Fuck that. Is the mess still open?"

"Only for men going out on ambush."

"What about men coming back from being ambushed?"

"The chaplain's tent is always open."

"Wise ass."

○

On reaching the command tent, Thomas ordered two troopers to carry Doll's body to the medical area. Then he dismissed us and he went inside to make his report. Some of the troopers hustled off to the mess to try and scrounge some hot food. The others wearily trudged off to their tents to get a night's sleep before tomorrow's war.

I found myself alone, watching Blondy's figure retreating toward the tent area. I was physically exhausted but mentally alert, my mind running through the events of the two days. I needed to talk to someone about them. I hurried after Blondy and caught up to him outside his tent.

"You got one more joint for me?" I asked. "I need it to settle down."

He grinned. "I could use one myself. But just one more and then you'll have to get your own supply. It's easy. Everybody's hustling the stuff."

Blondy led me around to the rear of his tent and we sat down on the ground. "I don't smoke out in the open except on patrol. There's a couple of hard-ass sergeants around here always looking to make life more miserable. I don't give them any help."

We lit up. The joint worked fine. It took my mind off my aching bones. We sat there in silence enjoying the cool night air. It was a refreshing relief after the steaming heat of the valley. With each drag the images of death and bloodshed slowly receded, leaving me in a hazy limbo of nothingness. It had a different effect on Blondy. From far off I heard his voice droning on. He was back in Cuntsville, the U.S. of A., reciting the pleasures of the flesh. I wasn't there with him.

After a while, he came back to Vietnam. "Thirty days, Glass. One fucking month. That's all I got to go."

"I hope you make it," I said.

"Hope, shit! You can bet your ass on it."

"Doll didn't make it."

"Fuck Doll. He had it coming. I ain't no butcher. You trying to worry me?"

"No. I didn't mean it that way. I want you to make it. You're okay."

Blondy grunted and we lapsed into silence again, sucking the last of our joints.

Finally, I asked: "What'd you mean, he had it coming?"

"I mean them butchers usually collect their dues. It happens time and again."

My interest sharpened. "The VC finally get them, huh?"

"VC, my ass." He lit another joint and passed it to me. "We'll share this one. I'm getting low."

I took a deep, slow drag and handed it back to him. "The VC got Doll."

He smiled slyly. "You got a lot to learn, Glass. And you got a lot a time to do it."

I grinned without malice. "You trying to worry me, Blondy?"

He shook his head, sucked the joint and then stared at it, burning down. "This stuff can blow your mind clear and clean, make you see things sharper than you are. Know what I mean? It do that to you?"

"Yeah." I was running ahead of him and waiting patiently for him to catch up.

He passed me the joint. "Finish it off. I don't need no more." He closed his eyes and leaned his head back against the corner tent pole and he talked: "I told you about friendly casualties, remember?"

"Yeah, I remember."

"Well, now you know."

"Know what?"

"Doll was a friendly casualty."

"How do you figure that?"

Blondy laughed to himself. "You heard what happened.

79

You saw the results. Put it together, Glass."

"You put it together."

"Sure. Doll went into the field after the VC, right? And Thomas went right after him, right? And then we heard a single round go off and then a quick burst. And Thomas comes back alone with his story and we go out to get Doll and what do we find?"

"What Thomas told us."

"Yeah, only not exactly the way he told it. Three gooks are dead, shot up to hell, but one of them's got an extra clean hole through his skull. I figure that was Doll getting his kicks. And then he got the back of his head blown off. I figure that was Thomas."

"How do you figure that?"

"I heard them shots, same as you. I can't tell a single round of an M-16 from a gook AK. But I know the burst of an M-16. That was an M-16. And Doll wasn't about to turn his back on a gook unless he was sure he was dead. Besides, the whole back of his head was shot away. You saw that. And you don't do that with a single bullet."

"Then Thomas murdered Doll?"

"Yeah. I figure Doll was going to pump the other two in the head when Thomas blasted him."

"Why?"

"Because Doll was a sadistic bastard and a prick. He let Thomas lay out there with the old man and then he weasled the command from Thomas and led us to the end of that fucking ravine for no goddamn good reason except he wanted to be a fucking hero. In Thomas's head it all added up and he picked his time. He's a shrewd bastard. He covered all the bases."

"But he killed one of his own."

"He killed a mean, sonofabitch butcher who led us into an ambush. What about the men who got killed because of Doll? Don't they count?"

"Sure they count. But Doll didn't kill them. There's a difference."

"I ain't bleeding for no Doll. We could of all been dead on account of him."

"And nobody's going to know what Thomas did but you and me?"

"Everyone of them troopers knows, unless it was their first patrol, like you. And them medics are going to know when they pick the steel out of Doll's skull. They know an M-16 bullet from an AK."

"And they're not going to say anything?"

"Nobody's going to say nothing. It ain't their concern. But you figured on spilling your mouth to the lieutenant, huh? I'll bet you're still sweating about that kid at the river."

I nodded.

"Shit, Glass. You're all fucked up. It's a good thing you talked to me."

"I had to talk to someone. How can you just live with it?"

"You got to live with it, kid, or you'll go crazy. I told you that."

"But it's wrong. Don't you understand?"

"I understand the system, man. You don't buck it or you go under."

"The system's got to be responsible for what it's doing."

"Like I said, Glass, you got a lot to learn. You go into the lieutenant with this story and you'll get shot down. They'll have you in a psycho ward faster'n you know what hit you. You want to jerk yourself off, go ahead. But you didn't see Thomas do nothing, did you? You ain't an eye-witness, are you? And if you were, they don't want to know it. You'd just be screwing up the machinery and nobody wants that. Nobody! This war's just a matter of killing. The whole idea is to kill more and get killed less until somebody decides it's enough. I got thirty more days, and then fuck them all."

"But what's Thomas telling the lieutenant?"

"Just what the lieutenant wants to hear. He'll make it real good."

"And Thomas gets off the hook?"

"What's your beef with Thomas? He's an okay guy. He does his job. He's no butcher."

81

"You're way ahead of me, Blondy."

"Yeah. Two hundred and thirty-three days. But you'll learn. Just put in your time, keep your mouth shut and tick off the days. This ain't your life. It's a long, fucking nightmare. When you wake up you'll forget it ever happened."

"I'll never forget these two days."

"You better, kid, or it'll destroy you."

O

After my talk with Blondy I was a changed man. I didn't see things his way but I saw them differently than I had on that first patrol. Blondy had a tough, practical view that I couldn't live with. But he was right about the system. Either you lived with it or you went under. In time, I learned to live with it but in my own way.

I often think about Blondy these days in my prison cell. I never saw him again after our talk. I heard he was transferred to another company. I did ask after him and somebody told me he'd completed his three hundred and sixty-five days and gone home. Up, up and away to Cuntsville, the U.S. of A. I sometimes wonder if he's read the papers and knows what's happened to me and what he thinks about it all. And sometimes I half expect that I'll hear from him, though I know it's a foolish expectation. I'm sure he's managed to forget it all ever happened and he's out there somewhere, still putting in his time and keeping his mouth shut. I hope so. He was an all right guy and I'm glad I never told him that Thomas saved his life that day in the ravine. He might never have forgotten that.

O

When I returned to my tent the night of that first patrol, my bunkmate was there, leafing through a girlie magazine. He had arrived at the camp with me three days before, fresh from the States. I've forgotten his name. I didn't have much time to know him. He seemed like a pleasant enough guy, anxiously awaiting his first combat assignment. I remember he put down his magazine when I entered the tent and watched me as I undressed. He waited patiently until I crawled into bed before he said anything.

"How did it go?" he asked finally.

I looked at his bright, rosy face eagerly studying me, and I thought about all that had happened to me since I had left him sleeping after Sergeant Stone had come into the tent.

"Haven't you been out yet?" I asked.

"I go out on patrol tomorrow morning. What's it like?"

"Rough."

"Yeah. I heard about it. We got reports. You guys got shot up pretty bad I hear."

"Yeah."

"But *you* made it."

"I was lucky. Don't worry. Just do what you're told and you'll be okay."

"The VC are tough, huh?"

"Yeah."

"Tell me what happened?"

What could I tell him? About the boy on the riverbank? About Sergeant Stone getting blown up and decapitated? About slicing off fingers and ears and toes? About getting ambushed? About Doll? About Thomas? About my friend Blondy? How could it help him?

"I'm awfully tired," I said. "I haven't slept in two days."

"I'm sorry," he said.

"Listen, kid." I smiled to myself at calling him "kid." He was my age but minus my two days on patrol. It made an immense difference, didn't it? "You smoke grass?"

"Sure."

"Good. You use it on patrol. It's your best weapon against Charlie."

"Is it allowed?"

"Yeah. Out in the field it's part of your equipment. It'll get you through the shakes."

83

"Thanks."

"Sure. You'll be okay." I closed my eyes, and despite the thoughts whirling in my head I fell asleep quickly.

He was gone when I awoke the next morning. That night his patrol came back without him. A sniper had gotten him with a single round in the head. An evac chopper took him to his coffin.

I wish I could remember his name.

6.

I did not keep my resolution to report the senseless slaughter of the boy. After all that had happened on the patrol, the death of the boy was diminished in the scale of events. Still, I regretted my silence and to this day I carry the guilt of it. Perhaps if I had spoken out, things might have gone differently. Though I honestly don't think so. At the time I said nothing because I had no faith that attention would be paid to so small a death among so many deaths. But mostly I worried about the consequences to me if I accused a dead soldier whose body had been mutilated by the enemy. In the end, concern for my own safety dominated my troubled conscience. Today, considering all that has happened to me, I find it ironic that I'm still plagued by that failure to speak out—to put on the record the facts of that boy's death. By keeping silent, knowing the others would keep silent, I denied the existence of his life. Who would know what had become of that boy? No one.

Not so with our dead. They were all accounted for. By nightfall of the day after our return to camp, the results of Corporal Thomas's account of the mission were common knowledge:

Sergeant Stone, missing in action (who wants a decapitated body?) while risking his life in an enemy minefield to protect the lives of his patrol, was nominated posthumously for a Bronze Star.

Corporal Doll, killed in action while attacking an enemy position without regard for his own safety, was nominated posthumously for a Bronze Star and recommended for promotion to sergeant.

The gunship crew, missing in action, and the troopers, killed and wounded in action, were recommended for a Presidential Citation for destroying an entrenched enemy position in the face of overwhelming odds.

Corporal Thomas made a good case. His report contained the essentials to which Lieutenant Caldron added the embellishments necessary to satisfy the unwritten military code. Whenever possible don't ship a body home without a medal. Whenever possible don't list an MIA without a special commendation.

"Medals soothe the bereaved family, lieutenant. Commendations enhance the funeral ceremony. The army's got to keep up morale at home as well as here. It's the only way we'll get this rotten job done. You understand, lieutenant?"

"Yes sir, I understand fully."

Yessir, Lieutenant Caldron understood fully. And so did Corporal Jefferson Thomas, who made his report, and my friend Blondy, who kept his mouth shut. And now, so did I understand fully.

But the army is a sensitive machine ever alert to the threats against it. In the days that followed, it heard the troopers' grumbling criticism of Doll's leadership; it heard about the panic in the ravine and the near mutinous action of the troopers; it heard the ugly rumors that the medics had picked American steel from Doll's shattered skull. And the army sifted that information and then acted on it.

Within a week, all of the troopers of the two squads in the ravine were transferred separately to other combat units. And Blondy, as I said, was transferred to another outfit. Corporal Thomas was rewarded with an assignment to a rear area where it wasn't necessary for him to bear arms. Of all the men who participated in the action in that ravine, only I remained at Cam Binh in the Central Highlands.

O

Two weeks after the success of our mission, Intelligence reported the VC back in the ravine stockpiling fresh supplies. No further action was taken to dislodge them. Instead, our maps were re-marked to include the ravine as a fortified enemy position along with the western hills. Thereafter, the Army directed its patrols elsewhere.

Months later, after I was long gone from the Central Highlands, the base at Cam Binh came under direct rocket and artillery fire from the ravine and VC units stormed the camp by night. The siege was broken after two weeks. Our losses were among the heaviest in the war. I read the newspaper accounts with special interest. One story described the battle as "a shining example of American resistance under siege that will go down in the annals of our military history along with the Battle of the Bulge and the Alamo."

Subsequently, Cam Binh was considered of no strategic value and our forces were withdrawn.

Amen.

O

The routine of search-and-destroy patrols in the valley kept me occupied fully and the events and the men of that first patrol receded to the back of my mind. Every patrol is potentially hazardous and demands constant alertness. I learned that early and fast became a tough, hardened foot soldier. I did my job and kept to myself. It didn't pay to get too friendly. Relationships didn't last very long in Vietnam. My brief friendship with Blondy had taught me that. I missed him in those first days after his transfer. I had no one to bitch to and lean on. And to my surprise, I missed Thomas too. He had a solidity and a sense of himself that

87

I never came across again during my hitch. Without them, I felt vulnerable and I realized that my own survival depended solely upon myself. It's lonely when you detach yourself from your buddies, but it frees you from personal concern and anguish and keeps you from going crazy when you watch men die. Still, I never got used to the killing. I simply survived it somehow and went on.

Those early weeks of patrol were not routine as I had experienced it. They were unusually quiet. We stayed clear of the ravine. We did not encounter the enemy. We discovered minefields but lost no men. We came across VC caves but they were empty. We came upon peasants in black pajamas tilling the fields and the rice paddies. They were not hostile and we left them alone.

After a while, the absence of the enemy in the valley greatly improved my morale. I considered myself lucky to have stayed on at Cam Binh. It was turning out to be a quiet area where the lines were drawn, and if neither side overstepped them there was no conflict. That suited me fine. I could easily have endured my time in tramping through that hot valley by day and sleeping away my nights on that cool plateau. But it did not last. Nothing is constant in Vietnam except the heat. There are only interludes. My interlude of quiet days ended one morning at the edge of the village a mile north of the spot where Sergeant Stone had murdered the boy. I thought of him for the first time in three weeks because he had told us he came from there. Up to that time, our patrols had gone south. Now our orders were to investigate the village itself. There were reports of VC infiltration to secure food and to terrorize the villagers for cooperating with the Americans. The villagers were considered friendly to us, and though there had been small firefights in the vicinity, there had been no indication of VC support in the village itself.

Before we set out, Lieutenant Caldron briefed us personally to make it clear that our mission was extremely delicate. We were to investigate the extent of VC harassment without antagonizing the villagers. Their continued friendliness was essential to the security of the base. Moreover, the village was considered a model example of our old pacification program and our new Vietnamization policy. One of the troopers asked what the difference was. The lieutenant put him down sharply: "Don't be a wise ass! This isn't a question-and-answer session. It's a briefing. Just listen."

He addressed most of his remarks directly to the patrol leader, Sergeant Ecks, a cautious, conservative veteran, respected for protecting his men. I'd been in the field with him before. He had shown a firm, fatherly attitude toward his men and a diplomatic handling of the officers. As a result, he was well-liked by both sides—a rarity among NCO's.

"Sergeant Ecks, you know that village as well as anyone on this base," Lieutenant Caldron said. "That's why I picked you to lead this patrol. We want to know if the villagers are scared and why. We want to know if Charlie's taking their rice. We want to know if they're harboring Charlie. If Charlie has infiltrated we've got to get him out of there without alarming the villagers. We need their good will. That's a tall order, I know. It means you've got to get your information without hurting those people. I don't want anyone beating on them or threatening them with his M-16. Remember, they're our allies." Caldron glowered at the troopers. "Don't smirk. I know what you're thinking but we're not about to level that village. We've got to live with it as long as we maintain this base. That's the way it is. So you guys go easy. No blasting. If you spot any VC in the fields you don't fire unless they do *first*. In the village, you don't use your weapons at all unless you're openly attacked. If anybody fucks up, battalion headquarters will have your ass on the line. I got my orders. You're looking for information and signs—like fear among the villagers, or weapons, any young gooks hiding in the hootches, anything that looks suspicious. If you pick up any suspects, you bring them back here for questioning. And no rough stuff. We'll do all the interrogating."

"One point, lieutenant."

"What is it, sergeant?"

"If we do round up anybody we can't drag them around with us until we get back. It wouldn't look good holding anyone in that village too long. I know them people."

"Good point. Take any suspects to the field, away from the hamlet, and call in. We'll send an armed truck to pick them up. Any more questions? Okay, then get started. I want you back here by dark."

○

We took the main road out of the base. It wound down from the plateau through rock formations to the edge of the village at the north end of the valley. Normally, the road was heavily trafficked with trucks carrying supplies and transferring troops, but it was only eight o'clock and the trucks didn't start out until nine. By that time we would reach the village. It was less than an hour's march, all downhill. Still, we sweated every step of the way. It was hot and the road was dry. We kicked up swirls of dust as we marched and it coated our hands and faces. There was no such thing as a pleasant walk in Vietnam, not for foot soldiers.

There were six of us in the patrol, walking in pairs. Sergeant Ecks and his number two man, a corporal, were in the lead, then two troopers and then me and another trooper. I didn't know any of them except the sergeant. When we were halfway down the road and could see the village below us, the sight of it started my partner talking. He said his name was Hammer and I told him mine was Glass. He laughed at that and I had to smile. He was a big, beefy man who looked more like a pudding than a hammer. He grumbled about the lieutenant's briefing instructions. Hammer had his own ideas about pacifying a village that might have VC in it. You blasted it first and investigated later, and the more he talked the more his name suited his personality if not his appearance. He told me that the last time he had searched a "friendly" hamlet his best buddy had been killed by a VC hiding in one of the hootches. Hammer said he spotted the gook trying to

90

escape and he got him with a single shot. In the hootch he found his buddy dead from knife stabs.

"A young girl was lying on the floor crying like a fucking banshee. I figured she was the gook's girl and had been the bait that got my buddy. He wasn't the kind of guy to be taken by surprise. He was a careful bastard. But that cunt must have got to him. She was a real good-looker even in them dirty pajamas. Another time I could have put it to her myself but not with my buddy lying there. She was crying at me when I gave her half my clip right across her tits. That pacified her for good." The anger in his eyes subsided. "He was my best buddy. We'd put in nine months together. That was nearly two months ago. He'da been going home in three weeks. We had plans to stick together in the States. Maybe go into business together. He had a real head for business."

I looked at him but said nothing. He misunderstood my silence for sympathy.

"It don't pay to make friends in this shithole," he said. "Nothing good lasts in this fucking war. Nothin'."

At that, I agreed and he grinned at me. "Listen, Glass, I don't know how much time you got out here but don't never go into any of them hootches alone."

"Yeah."

"We got to stick together—help each other."

"Yeah."

"Hammer and Glass. That's pretty good."

He was looking for a replacement for his dead buddy but he couldn't know yet that I wasn't it.

O

We reached the hamlet around nine o'clock. At that hour, children were playing in the dirt of the road. They quickly gave up their games and gathered around us with hands outstretched, begging for food and candy. We had nothing much to give them and Sergeant Ecks shooed them away. But they trailed after us in the hope they would be given something, anything. Finally, I pulled a can of

91

C-rations from my rucksack and threw it far down the road behind me and the children scampered after it. The sergeant looked at me with disapproval. Beside me, Hammer sneered and called me a sucker. I ignored him.

As we moved along, the only adults we saw were very old men. They stood about idly in front of their hootches or squatted in the dust of their doorways. They stared at us with the empty eyes of the aged who have seen the bitterness of life and are resigned to it. I wondered what thoughts went on behind those tired, worn faces. What did they think of this endless war that raged around them? Their lives were so simple, spent entirely in their village and the surrounding fields. What did they think of the strangers invading their hamlet? How could they comprehend the traffic of the choppers knifing through their blue sky, the tanks and half-tracks churning up their green fields, the armed patrols sloshing through their rice paddies as they tilled the earth? I had read that most of the people in the remote hamlets did not know the name of their president or the seat of their government. In the States we knew both and we were here to spread the word though they could not understand us nor we them. But they understood the language of guns, and when we marched past their straw hootches they smiled at us. It was their only means of protection.

Sergeant Ecks had decided to begin our investigation in the marketplace. It was the center of activity in the hamlet, and at that early hour it was bustling with activity. Both the vendors and buyers, carrying on a flourishing trade, were women. There was not a man in sight. It was a typical village scene. All the able-bodied men were absent, either in the South Vietnam armed forces or fighting with the Vietcong, or somewhere out of sight. Any man of military age not in uniform was suspicious to both sides and was visible to his family only after nightfall when he was safe from American scrutiny and had only the VC to fear.

We held our rifles in readiness as we filtered through the marketplace. The women merchants and shoppers paid us no attention. American patrols were a part of their daily life and they appeared untroubled by our presence. At one end of the market, outside one of the hootches, a funeral was in progress and there was a good deal of crying and wailing. The deceased, an old man, was laid out on a wooden table surrounded by burning candles on poles that released thick curls of smoke. The family and friends of the dead man, all women except for two or three old men, sat cross-legged on the ground in a series of semicircles. From time to time one or another of the women shrieked aloud in grief but no one tried to comfort her. It seemed to me that as one mourner's wail diminished another took it up like a ritual for the dead. It was a strange sight to witness a funeral amidst the commerce of a marketplace. And yet it was not so strange in this country where death and life existed in closer proximity than I had ever known it.

We started to move on through the market when Hammer hesitated, his attention drawn by the group of mourners closest to the dead man. After peering intently at them, he drew Sergeant Ecks aside and whispered to him. I watched the sergeant study the mourners and I followed his gaze. Five women in black, heads bowed, were moaning and chanting. Every few moments one or another of them threw her head back and lamented in a loud wail. Only the one in the center, a smaller figure whose face was hidden under a black mantle, remained still and silent.

"It's a man, I tell you," Hammer said to the sergeant loud enough for the rest of us to hear. "I saw his face before. He's maybe seventeen, eighteen years old. That gook's military age. I'll prove it to you."

The rest of us pressed around the sergeant, who was shaking his head. "No. Let's just watch for a while. You two." He pointed at the two troopers who had marched ahead of me. "Go around to the other side of this group and keep your eyes open. I don't want you to do anything unless there's trouble. And I don't want anyone getting trigger-happy. If that's a gook, we'll take him quietly. Just be careful if he tries to make a run for it. You got that?"

The troopers nodded and wandered away to the opposite side of the funeral group and took up positions where they could observe the front row of mourners.

The four of us stood about idly under a tree a few yards from the funeral. Sergeant Ecks lit a cigarette and offered his pack to us. Everyone accepted but me. I wanted to smoke a joint to ease the tightness developing in my chest but I restrained myself. I hadn't smoked any grass the one time I was out with the sergeant and I didn't know how he felt about it. He ran things by the book and I didn't want to cross him in any way.

After a few minutes of watching the mourners, Hammer grew impatient. "We going to stand around here all day, sarge? Why don't we just grab him and see if I'm right?"

"We can't barge into their ceremony. It would turn the whole village against us. You heard the lieutenant."

"Shit, sarge. We're here to find ginks, ain't we?"

"Yeah. Only we ain't sure he's a VC. We don't even know it ain't a woman under that shroud."

"Woman, my ass. He's sitting right there like a mummy. How come he ain't swaying and screaming like the rest of them?"

"That's what we're waiting to find out."

"This fucking funeral could last for hours," Hammer complained. "I seen them howl like that all day."

The sergeant's eyes narrowed. "If that's a VC he ain't going to stay put there with us watching. He'll do something before long. We just have to wait for it."

Hammer looked disgusted but he didn't answer.

The corporal said, "I can't figure why Charlie would sit at a funeral in broad daylight with patrols going through."

"Maybe the stiff's his father," Hammer said. "Wouldn't you take a chance if it was your old man's funeral?"

"Not me." The corporal grinned. "I hate my old man."

Hammer started to say something but stopped. One of the women, who had been lamenting the loudest, suddenly got to her feet beside the still, black figure and stood over the dead man and sobbed heavily. Finally, she composed herself and leaned forward and kissed the sunken cheek of the dead man. Then she turned abruptly and slipped through the group of mourners and walked off into the market.

"Where the hell's she going?" Hammer said excitedly.

"Maybe she's going to do her shopping," the corporal said and he smiled at Hammer. I smiled with him.

"It ain't funny," Hammer said. "I think we should follow her." He was looking toward one of the nearby stalls where the woman had stopped and was talking to another woman.

"Yeah," Sergeant Ecks said to Hammer. "See where she goes but don't do nothing stupid. Get back here as soon as you know. We'll be waiting."

Hammer started after her and I watched as he approached the vegetable stall and stood there a few feet away from the woman.

"He likes playing detective," the corporal said.

"Yeah," the sergeant said. "But he just might have something. I don't think that's a woman squatting there neither but it could be just a kid. Maybe the stiff's grandson. Kids don't know how to cry at funerals. We'll just watch a little more. It ain't ten o'clock yet. We got time."

I liked the sergeant's calm approach to the situation. It surprised me. The average patrol leader would have disrupted the funeral ceremony without regard for the people. Ecks showed a sensitivity in a brutalized atmosphere. It was refreshing.

After five minutes or so, Hammer returned looking puzzled. The woman had reappeared and taken her place on the ground beside the bier and resumed her mournful crying as if she were acting a role. The whole setting, the pageantry of the marketplace, the ritual of the funeral before a GI audience, was bizarre. Even in this strange war it was a unique experience for me. I was fascinated and disturbed, anticipating a climax I could not foresee.

"What happened?" Sergeant Ecks asked Hammer.

"I followed her through the market. She talked to some women and then came back." He shrugged in bewilderment. "I can't figure it out. Now she's bawling again over that stiff."

"We're wasting our time," the corporal said. "It's just a fucking gook funeral. What's there to figure out?"

Hammer's face flushed. "You seen any young guys in this whole village? The only one is sitting on his ass right by that corpse. I saw his face. I can smell a VC. I'm telling you that's Charlie. If the sarge says to get him I'll bet even money he makes a break for it." Hammer looked at the sergeant.

"We can't risk it. So far this village is peaceful. I want to keep it that way. I don't want any killing."

"What the hell are you worried about," Hammer said, his patience running out. "We can handle all these fucking gooks."

"Yeah, only we're going to handle them like I say. I don't want any more of your shit, Hammer."

Hammer didn't get the chance to reply. A series of piercing screams rang out from somewhere behind us in the market and several of the women began to scurry in that direction, drawing our attention toward the disturbance. Even the mourners were distracted and ceased their wailing and craned their heads to see what was happening. Sergeant Ecks yelled at the two troopers to investigate the outburst. With their rifles fixed they moved quickly into the market and disappeared in the crowd of women fleeing in every direction. At the height of the commotion, I noticed the small black figure at the bier spring to his feet and scoot under the platform holding the dead man and disappear into the nearby hootch. Sergeant Ecks and Hammer had spotted him, too. "Get him," the sergeant commanded. Responding quickly for such a heavy man, Hammer dashed through the circle of mourners and reached the entrance to the hootch, where he stopped and cautiously pointed his rifle at the opening. When he saw I was right behind him, he went in. I followed. In contrast to the sunlight and noise in the market, it was dark and very quiet inside the hootch. Straw mats covered the dirt floor and a small wooden table and two chairs were the only furniture. After a moment's scrutiny, Hammer said, "He must have crawled under the straw wall." He rushed out through the doorway and around to the back of the hootch. By the time I caught up with him, he was pointing across the field that bordered the village. "There he goes."

A small dark figure less than thirty meters off was running through the low, cultivated green field.

"We'll never catch him," I said, but Hammer had no thought of chasing after him. He raised his rifle and fired it. In the same instant, the small figure tumbled forward in the grass out of sight.

"Got the mother," Hammer exclaimed and he ran toward his prey. Directed by the sound of moaning, we approached cautiously. And there he was, a young boy, perhaps fourteen, lying on his back, his hand clutching a shoulder covered with blood, his small black eyes staring with fright up at us. He made an effort to sit up when Hammer placed his boot on the boy's chest and thrust him back against the earth and held him there. "You little motherfucker. You didn't fool me in that funeral shroud. Say your goddam prayers, Charlie. You ain't going to kill any more of my buddies."

The boy closed his eyes.

"What are you going to do?" I asked.

"Blow his fucking head off."

"But he's not armed. He didn't shoot at us. He's just a kid. The sarge told us to hold anyone for interrogation."

"Fuck the sarge. He didn't believe me when I told him this fucker wasn't a woman."

"But he's only a kid."

"He was trying to get away. Why was he running? He's a fucking VC."

"Let the lieutenant decide that."

"What the fuck's the matter with you?"

"I don't want to kill the kid. He can't hurt us. He's wounded. And if he's a VC they'll want to interrogate him. He can give us information."

Hammer, his beefy face oozing sweat, looked stunned by my outburst. "I seen kids like this shooting AK's. The fucker who got my buddy wasn't much older than this gink."

The boy twitched with pain and tried to shift his body under Hammer's boot. "Don't move, you little bastard," Hammer rasped and he jammed his boot harder against the boy's chest and slipped it up into his bloody shoulder. The boy whimpered and his dark eyes looked pleadingly at me. In his face I saw the same wild fear of the boy on the riverbank. Blood flowed up around his mouth.

"You're choking him!" I yelled. "Let him up." I looked hard at Hammer and controlled my anger. "The sarge will be coming any minute. He won't like it if you shoot the kid. He goes by the book. I been out with him before."

"So that's it," Hammer said tightly. "You're his asslicker."

"Yeah," I said, feeling the strength of my position. I clicked back the safety on my rifle. "I go by the book, too."

Hammer was sweating rivers but he managed a tight smile. "Okay." He removed his foot from the boy's shoulder. "I'll hold him here. Get the sarge. I'll wait for you."

I didn't trust him and I stalled, hoping the sergeant or one of the troopers would appear. But there was no one in sight. Finally I said, "Okay. I'll be back as fast as I can. Keep your cool."

"I'm always cool," Hammer said. He watched me as I retreated toward the village. I kept glancing back over my shoulder. Hammer just stood there staring at me. He rested his rifle in the crook of his arm and mopped his face with his sleeve. When I reached the hootch at the edge of the field and looked back once more, Hammer motioned to me to hurry. I turned the corner of the hootch, out of his sight, and kneeled down, pressing myself close against the wall of the hootch, and peered back at the field. I was sure Hammer couldn't see me. My whole body stiffened like a steel rod. Hammer was poking at the boy with his rifle. I waited and watched. The boy struggled to his feet, still gripping his shoulder, and with Hammer prodding him from behind he stumbled forward away from the village. I didn't understand. Why the hell was Hammer marching him off? It was directly against our orders. I started to get to my feet to stop Hammer when he fired his rifle. At that close range, the blast raised the boy off the ground and pitched him several feet forward into the grass. Hammer stood motionless, looking toward the village. I froze against the wall of the hootch. Somewhere behind me I heard women's voices shrieking. I didn't know if it was mourning at the funeral or alarm at the gunfire. I kept my eyes on Hammer as he cradled his rifle and lit a cigarette. He walked to the spot where the boy had fallen and stood there—waiting and smoking. The field was quiet and serene in the morning sun with only the figure of Hammer in it. Not until that moment had I realized that there were no villagers working in the fields—no witnesses but me.

I trembled with the sickening feeling of having again failed a moment of crisis. It immobilized me against the wall of the hootch. It was the sight of Hammer idly smoking that finally stirred me. A hatred for him rose like bile in my mouth. I got to my feet and ran into the market. Pressing through groups of women, gathered again around the vegetable stalls, I looked for the members of my patrol. They were nowhere about. At the far end of the marketplace I stopped to get my bearings and became aware that a cluster of women were staring anxiously at me. "Where are the Americans?" I shouted. They looked at me in bewildered silence. "Doesn't anybody in this fucking country understand English?" I was furious at my frustration. How the hell do you talk to your allies? How can you help them when they can't understand you? I gazed into the frightened, sullen faces of those simple women. One of them could be the mother of that dead boy in the field. Isolated in that market, I felt like the victim in a ludicrous nightmare with death mocking the absurdity of life. Suddenly I was brought back to the reality of my situation. One of the women raised her hand and pointed toward a hootch at the end of the market square. With a grateful nod, I turned away and went to the hootch. Outside the entrance I hesitated, remembering Hammer's remark about not entering a hootch alone. From inside I heard the familiar sound of GI English, "Let's get the fuck out of here," and the corporal appeared in the doorway.

"Where the hell you been?" he asked, stepping outside.

"Where's the sergeant?"

"He's coming out."

I heard some jabbering in Vietnamese in the hootch and Sergeant Eck's voice saying, "Yeah, yeah." Then the two other troopers, followed by the sergeant, joined us outside.

"What happened, Glass?" the sergeant asked. "Did you get him? We heard a shot?"

I nodded, collecting my thoughts. "What happened here?"

"Nothing. One of them old gook women had some kind of fit in the market and fainted and they all started screaming. She's inside. I can't make nothing out of their gook talk. The heat must have got to her." He mopped his forehead as if to underline his remark. "What was the shooting?"

"The boy was running through the field. He was getting away when Hammer fired at him. He winged him in the shoulder." I didn't want to answer more than I was asked in front of the others. I didn't know them. When I could get the sergeant alone I planned on telling him everything. Hammer didn't know what I'd seen. I had to be cautious but this time there would be no keeping silent. I'd made up my mind when I'd looked into the frightened faces of those women in the market. Life wasn't ludicrous and death wasn't abstract.

"Where's Hammer?"

"He's guarding the boy. He doesn't look more than fourteen. I came back to get you."

"Good," Sergeant Ecks said. "Let's go."

○

On the way to the field, Sergeant Ecks expressed concern about the situation. He suspected a connection between the woman fainting in the market and the boy trying to escape. It had the smell of a scheme to him. He suggested that the kid was possibly a VC being protected by the villagers or at least by some of them. The corporal and the two troopers were quick to agree with him. Why else had the boy risked his life to get away if he wasn't guilty? I could think of several reasons but I didn't raise them. It was possible they could be right but I wanted more evidence and less speculation. Yet even if the boy was a VC it didn't justify Hammer's killing him. I couldn't see it for anything else but murder and against official orders at that.

Hammer, standing where I'd last seen him, waved to us as we approached across the field.

"Where's the gook?" Sergeant Ecks asked me.

"Lying in the grass, I guess." I wondered what his reaction would be when he found the boy dead. It came quickly enough.

Seeing the boy lying at Hammer's feet, his eyes and mouth open in death, Ecks said to me, "I thought he was only wounded in the shoulder."

"He was alive when I left to get you."

"What happened, Hammer?"

"The fucker tried to get away. I had to blast him."

"You telling me he was wounded in the shoulder and he tried to run for it with you standing over him?"

"Ain't nothing wrong with his legs, sarge. I had my rifle on my shoulder and was lighting a cigarette. Next thing I knew he was running through the grass."

"Since when do you guard a gook with your rifle in the sling?"

"I guess I wasn't thinking. What's the big deal? It's just another dead gook."

101

"You were supposed to keep him alive for interrogation. We don't even know if he's a VC. He don't look more'n thirteen."

"He's old enough, sarge. Them little fuckers know how to handle an AK. I been up against kids younger than him."

"Yeah. Only he didn't have no AK, did he?"

"No."

"Too bad. It would have helped your case."

"What case? You saw him trying to get away. You said 'get him.' I got him."

"Roll him over."

The corporal kneeled and turned the body face down. There was a gaping bullet hole at the base of the head just below the hairline.

"That's a real clean job of shooting, Hammer," the sergeant said. "And the gook was scrambling through the grass, huh?"

"Yeah. But he didn't get very far. Maybe ten meters by the time I got my rifle off my shoulder and fired."

"A single round, huh?"

"That's all I needed. When I hit him in the shoulder he was thirty meters into the field and he ain't very big." Hammer looked pleased with himself. "I was the best marksman in my whole fucking battalion."

"Especially at ten meters, and maybe less, huh?"

Hammer didn't reply.

The sergeant looked around at all of us. "We're going back into that village and continue checking. I'm sure them villagers have been watching us right now. And when they find that gook they ain't going to like us much. You understand? If this kid's clean they can make a stink about it." He looked at Hammer. "I just hope he ain't the son of some village elder."

"Shit, sarge," Hammer said. "I'm just a GI, not a politician. I'm supposed to kill gooks, ain't I?"

"You're supposed to obey orders. Your fucking story don't hold water. There ain't a GI in Nam who'd believe that kid was trying to escape with a hole in his shoulder."

"You saying I'm a liar?"

"I'm saying you're full of shit, Hammer, and I'd throw the book at you if I had a single witness."

Hammer was stunned. "I don't understand this fucking war. I do my job. I kill gooks like they trained me and now you're telling me I'm wrong."

"I'm telling you you had a wounded runaway and you fucked up. Maybe you just turned that whole village against us. I don't know. I hope not. Now let's get back there. It don't look good standing out here."

"What about that gook woman who was sitting next to Charlie at the funeral?" Hammer asked anxiously. "You find her? Maybe she knows something."

"Yeah, I thought about that. Let's find out."

On the way back across the field I thought only about the opportunity to tell Sergeant Ecks he had a single witness. I didn't know when the opportunity would come but I nurtured it. Hammer watched me with suspicion but I gave him no indication that he had anything to worry about. Secretly I was immensely relieved. If Sergeant Ecks was prepared to go by the book, he was my man.

O

Though the funeral was still in progress, the woman was no longer among the mourners at the bier and our chances of finding her in the village were slight. None of us was that certain of her identity, and in a village of middle-aged Vietnamese women all of whom looked a good deal alike to us our search was less than promising. The language barrier greatly frustrated our efforts at interrogation, and if any of the natives understood English they concealed it. In his anxiety, Hammer kept seeing the woman in almost every face in the market and he approached several and questioned them harshly. Each time the woman regarded him with bewilderment and fear and kept silent. An undercurrent of hostility toward us became apparent and more and more of the women drifted out of the market and returned to their hootches. Finally Sergeant Ecks called a halt to our efforts to find the woman. Our presence was disturbing to the villagers. We had created a tense atmosphere in the normally bustling routine of the market.

Still, we had our orders and Sergeant Ecks was not a man not to carry them out. If our search of the marketplace had come to naught, perhaps our search of the hootches might be more fruitful. We proceeded with it, going from hut to hut. But the hootches turned up no weapons, no unusual concern in the faces of the old men and their women—at least none that we could detect. There was only resignation at our unwanted presence. They endured the search of their homes in silence. If they hid something from us, we did not find it. They were inscrutable, knowing they would remain here in their homes tilling a life from their fields long after we were gone with our planes and our tanks and our guns. Yet they would remember us long after we had forgotten them. We were a harsh reality in their world; they were a nightmare in ours—a nightmare that measured 365 days—and when it ended we would go home and resume our lives as if it had never happened.

By early afternoon, we had searched more than half the hootches and turned up nothing. None of the natives complained to us of VC harassment. On the contrary, when we mentioned the VC, the one word they readily understood, they shrugged and shook their heads. Some of the women, who understood a few words of English, were more positive. Like a dirge, they repeated: "No VC here."

It seemed pointless to me to continue the search. The whole village was alerted to it. But Sergeant Ecks was patient and doggedly thorough and insisted we check every hootch in the hamlet. With several hours of daylight remaining, he had no intention of short-cutting the job, dull and distasteful as it was. He didn't like going into those hootches and disrupting those people but it had to be done. Orders were orders. You carried them out.

It was four o'clock when we came out of the last hootch and took a break to smoke. We were all more weary than if we had been in a firefight. Aside from the debilitating heat, the hours of frustrating effort to communicate had exhausted us. The corporal was disappointed that we hadn't turned up anything but the sergeant was satisfied with the operation. We'd been thorough in our search and he was convinced the villagers were not intimidated by Charlie or we would have detected some sign of it.

Though nothing more had been said about the killing of the boy since we had left the field, an unspoken edginess existed among us. During our search, Hammer had appeared troubled and kept warily eying the sergeant and me. It was apparent that the sergeant's tough response to his story had him worried but he had been careful not to arouse him further. I sensed that he didn't know what to make of me. If he had any suspicion that I had seen the killing, he suppressed it. But I was aware that he stayed close to me, and if I said something to the sergeant he was always within earshot. He sweated a lot and I knew it wasn't simply due to the heat, and while I found myself secretly enjoying his uneasiness it scared me. I had learned enough in the field to know that guys like Hammer would do almost anything to protect themselves. Like starving wolves, they would eat their own. In my own way, I was ready to do the same when the time came.

We made a final tour of the marketplace before returning to the base. Buyers and vendors were gone. The vegetable stalls were empty, closed for the day. The funeral mourners, with the dead man they mourned, had departed for the burial place, leaving behind the candles, still flickering and smoking. There was no further purpose in our remaining there and we started back toward the base, taking a path along the edge of the field that skirted the village. We had only gone a few meters when we saw two of the village elders coming toward us from the fields. They walked very slowly and with difficulty, bent under the strain of the burden they were carrying. It was the dead boy. The old men held their heads bowed and breathed heavily with each step. Not until they were abreast of us

105

did they look up and stare silently into our faces. As they passed, I shook my head sadly at them.

"I think we should question them," Hammer said. "They might know something about Charlie."

"Maybe they'd like to question us," the sergeant said. "You want to answer their questions?"

"I just did my fucking job."

"Yeah. Only I don't think they'd understand that even if you knew gook talk. They're just two old men taking a dead kid home."

"They're used to that, sarge. The country's full of dead gooks. And dead GI's, sarge."

"I don't need no lecture, Hammer. I've done my fair share of killing gooks. That's how I got these stripes."

"Then what the hell you picking on me for?"

"Because you fucked up."

"You wanted me to let that gook get away?"

"I wanted you to hold him prisoner. That's what we came here for, to take suspects. If you can't guard a four-teen-year-old kid with a bullet in his shoulder, you ain't the man for the job."

"He'da gotten clean away if I hadn't hit him with that first shot."

"You want another medal for your marksmanship?"

"Shit. I don't understand you."

"Then shut your ass and move it. Let's go."

I was enormously heartened by the sergeant's attitude and all the way back to the base I thought only about the moment when I could tell him what I knew. I was going to answer the question I saw in the faces of those two old men.

○

"Why didn't you tell me before I made my report to the lieutenant?" Sergeant Ecks asked, scowling at me. It was eight o'clock in the evening and we had been talking for more than half an hour in the mess tent. The others in the patrol had finished their meal and left. The sergeant had joined us late and I had lingered over a cup of coffee to get him alone. Hammer had stayed around long enough to find out what the sergeant had told the lieutenant. Ecks had made him squirm a bit before admitting he'd reported Hammer's account of the killing. As far as Hammer was concerned that closed the book on the day's patrol. Now I had reopened it.

"I couldn't talk in front of Hammer could I? I had to get you alone."

"I figured it that way the minute I saw the hole in the kid's head. It had to be fired from about three, maybe four feet. But I had no proof the kid wasn't running. It was bullshit but I had no proof."

"You have now. I'm your witness."

"It ain't that simple."

"Why not?"

"I already told the lieutenant Hammer's story. Only I made it better."

"Why'd you do that?"

"I couldn't go with his half-assed story and I couldn't go by the book without the facts. So I back up my men irregardless of my suspicions. You can't run a good operation by knifing your own men unless you got the facts. You ruin morale and then you got a bunch of fuckups on your hands with everybody out for themselves."

"But you said yourself Hammer fucked up. Now you got facts to prove it."

"No can do, Glass. How'd it look going back to the lieutenant after I'd made a good case for Hammer?"

"You tell him the truth. You just found out from me. I'm ready to go with you if you want."

"He's gonna ask why you waited. It'll look bad. My report's a matter of record now."

"They can change the fucking record. I told you I didn't want to talk with Hammer around. I'll tell that to the lieutenant."

"That's going to make me look lousy. I really bullshitted the lieutenant good about how the kid got it. It made sense."

Now I scowled. "What the hell did you tell the lieutenant?"

"That Hammer killed the kid with his first shot when he was running away in that field."

"But there were two shots."

"The lieutenant don't know that."

"But the whole patrol does."

"So what?"

"So what if the lieutenant finds out there were two shots?"

"Why should he find out? He's got no reason to ask questions. And who's going to tell him different?"

I was amazed. "You made a better case for Hammer than he did for himself."

"He had no choice. I did."

"I don't get it."

"I told you. Without proof, I couldn't nail Hammer." He grinned. "I had to protect the patrol."

"You were protecting your own ass because Hammer didn't follow your orders."

The sergeant's face hardened. "It's finished. I got nothing more to say about it."

"It's not finished. I'm going to the lieutenant."

"Don't stick your neck out, kid. It'll get chopped off."

"Shit! If you had a witness, you said. I thought you meant it."

"I did mean it. Only now it's too late."

"It's not too late for me."

"You gonna make me out a liar?"

"I'm not going to make you out anything. I'm going to tell what I saw, that's all."

"The lieutenant will have us all in on the carpet. It'll be your word against ours."

"Nobody saw nothing but me."

"How about Hammer? He killed the kid and I put it on

108

the record how he did it. Hammer'll back me up and so will the others. You better believe it."

"You're crazy!"

"Like a fox, Glass. I said what I said because I had nothing else to go on. I ain't changing that story now. And nobody's going to fuck me up. You understand?"

"Is that a threat, sarge?"

"It's the facts of life." His voice softened. "I'da hit Hammer with the book if you'da come to me sooner. You know that. But now it's a different story. It wouldn't do nobody any good to change it and it'd make us all look bad. It's a stinking situation and I don't like it any more'n you do. I know guys like Hammer. They live for killing. That ain't good soldiering in my book and I don't like seeing them get away with it. But I ain't going to let them ruin my army career. I ain't just putting in my time here. I'm in this army for keeps. I got a good record and everybody knows me for a fair joe. It ain't right for a fuckup like Hammer to spoil it. You can bet your ass he won't pull nothing like this again on me."

Suddenly, I felt sorry for him. All his strength had collapsed. I would never have believed he would become an accomplice to Hammer's act. But that no longer troubled me. What did trouble me was that he was making me an accomplice as well. I resisted.

"I can't keep my mouth shut, sarge."

"You want me to make a big deal over one gook kid who might be a VC?"

"It doesn't matter if he was a VC. What matters is we never got the chance to find out what he was. If we don't stop guys like Hammer from killing just for kicks, then we're guilty of the killing as much as he is."

"Bullshit! Hammer's guilty because he acted against orders."

"Yeah," I said tiredly. "It was against orders."

"Don't pull that on me, Glass. Following orders is what this army's all about. It's the way it is. You do your job and forget the rest of it."

I smiled weakly. "I'm always being told to forget it. Trouble is I got a long memory."

"I'm telling you to forget today, Glass. Sleep on it. It'll look different to you in the morning."

"That kid'll still be dead in the morning, sarge."

"You might be too, Glass."

"You going to knock me off, sarge?"

"Not tonight, Glass." The sergeant smiled. "But Charlie could rocket this base any time. He's just sitting over in them hills watching all the time."

"Yeah." I didn't smile.

"And then there's old Hammer. No telling what he might do if he heard you was talking to the lieutenant."

"Yeah. I thought about that. But I just might get him busted first."

"That wouldn't be no skin off my ass," the sergeant said, still grinning.

I got up from the table. "I'll sleep on it, sarge. I'll keep you informed."

"You do that, Glass. And think about what I said. The war ain't ending tomorrow. How much time you got left here?"

"I don't know, do I, sarge?" And I walked out of the mess tent, leaving him to think about that.

○

I spent the night smoking grass and in the morning I went to see the lieutenant.

○

When I had finished telling him the entire story, including my talk with the sergeant, the lieutenant leaned back in his chair and looked at me in silence. His face was composed, and if he was at all dismayed he did a good job of concealing it. I shifted uneasily in my chair, waiting for some kind of reaction.

"I'm glad you came to see me, Glass," he said finally.

110

"A company commander can't do his job right unless he knows what's happening with his men in the field."

I didn't know what to say to that so I just nodded.

"You're sure you're the only one who saw Hammer kill the boy?"

"Yes sir."

"None of the villagers saw it? Someone out in the fields?"

"No sir. There was no one in the field but Hammer and the kid."

"Didn't anyone hear that second shot?"

"I don't know, sir. They could have heard it in the village but they're used to hearing gunfire around here. No one pays much attention."

"Then no one came out of the village at the time?"

"No sir. At least not while I was hiding behind the hootch. But I didn't stay very long. I went looking for the sergeant. Someone could have seen Hammer standing in the field afterwards. I don't know. He stayed there until we got back."

"And then you were all there for some minutes?"

"Yes sir, until we went back and searched the hootches."

"Was anyone at the funeral worried about the boy missing?"

"I didn't stop to see. I was too anxious to find the patrol."

"Yes. But the funeral continued?"

"Yes sir."

"And the market was busy?"

"Yes sir."

"So if they heard the gunfire they weren't very disturbed about it."

"Not that I could tell."

"How long do you figure Hammer was waiting for you to return with the patrol?"

"Ten minutes, maybe fifteen."

111

"And how long did you stay in the field talking before you returned to the village?"

"Another ten minutes."

"And during that time did you notice any villagers watching you?"

"No sir."

His questions increased my discomfort. I hadn't expected a cross-examination as if I were on a witness stand. I sensed what he was getting at and I didn't like it.

"Would you say the villagers couldn't be sure who killed the boy?"

"No. I wouldn't say that. They've got a pretty good idea by now."

"Why do you say that?"

"They saw the boy make a run for it and they saw Hammer and me go after him. And they heard the first shot for sure. We were standing right near the hootch, maybe fifteen meters from the funeral."

"Right. But they couldn't know if anyone was hit or even what you were shooting at, could they?"

"Not right then. But they sure found out later when they found the body and brought it back."

"But they can't be certain who did it, can they?"

"Sir. I'm telling you Hammer did it. That's why I'm here."

"Yes, Glass. But right now I'm interested in what the villagers know."

"I think I understand, sir. But would you mind telling me what's on your mind? It might save time."

Lieutenant Caldron scowled at me but then thought better of it. "Yes. Perhaps you're right, Glass." He attempted a smile. "We are on the same side, aren't we?"

"Yes sir."

"I need this detailed information, Glass. My job isn't easy. I know how it looks to you, but I've got battalion headquarters to answer to and they'll want all the facts."

"I gave you all the facts, sir."

"There are small details that may seem irrelevant to you, Glass, but believe me they're not. This could blow up into something a lot bigger than you realize."

"Sir?"

"If that boy's not a VC and those villagers think we killed him, they could be up here pretty soon complaining to base headquarters. We don't want trouble with them. We need their friendship. It's my job to make a good case for us."

I felt the old tightness in my chest. "I don't see how you can make a case for us, sir."

"Why not, if nobody saw it but you?"

"Then you don't intend to pass on my information to battalion headquarters?"

"That may not be necessary, Glass. I don't think you understand the problem we're facing."

"I think I do, sir."

"No, you don't. What's done is done. We can't bring that boy back to life. I wish we could. We might find out why the hell he ran. But right now we've got to keep those villagers in line. That's the job I have to do now. I told your patrol this was a delicate mission. Now, because of Hammer's stupidity, it's more delicate and I'm glad to have the facts from you."

"Excuse me, sir, but those villagers know now that the boy was shot in the shoulder and in the back of the head. They can figure out what happened. They're not dumb."

"Yes, but until you came in here, *I* didn't know there were two shots. Those villagers would have had more facts than I had." He shook his head. "Sergeant Ecks should have leveled with me. I know he was covering for his men. I can't fault him for that. But he should have known better. He's been around. He knows how the chain of command operates. I'd have protected him but I can't cover if I don't have all the facts. I have to thank you for that, Glass. You understand?"

"But I didn't come here to cover it up, lieutenant."

"Now don't you worry about that, Glass. I'll handle everything. I just don't want any surprises and there won't be any, will there?"

"No sir. You've got the whole story."

"Good."

"What about Hammer, sir? When he finds out I've been here, he's not going to like it."

The lieutenant smiled. "I wondered when you'd get around to that. Now don't you worry. I'll handle Hammer and Sergeant Ecks. He'll be pissed, too, when he finds out."

"Yes sir. But I want you to know I came here knowing they'd be gunning for me afterwards."

"You did right, Glass. I'll protect you."

I hated myself for having turned the conversation around to my own safety. I had gone through that during the night when I'd made up my mind to speak out. I felt unclean and I rebelled against it.

"I can take care of myself, lieutenant," I blurted out.

"Yes. But I have to take care of morale around here. It's part of the job. You stay away from Hammer. I'll see you don't go out on any patrols with him."

"That'd suit me fine, sir."

"I don't want our little talk to get around, Glass. You understand? I wouldn't want it to get back to battalion headquarters. I'll handle that myself."

"Yes sir."

"Glass?"

"Sir?"

"Don't worry about that boy. I know how you feel. It makes me sick, too. But you've got to expect things like this in combat. The important thing is not to let it throw you."

"I'll be okay."

"Good. One more thing. Did Hammer cut the ears off the boy?"

"No sir. He wasn't touched after he was dead."

"That's good. If his ears had been sliced off it would

114

look really bad. The VC don't do that." I met the lieutenant's gaze. "That's all, Glass."

"Yes sir." I got up and left.

Outside the command tent I blinked from the glare of the morning light. I was disgusted with myself. I'd been had. The lieutenant had made me an accomplice to a murder I'd come to expose. If I went over his head to battalion headquarters my life wouldn't be worth shit.

○

At an army base, especially in a combat zone, it is difficult to keep information confidential. News finds a way of filtering down from the highest echelons to the lowest. And so it was, on the day following my talk with the lieutenant, that my platoon heard of the meeting between the elders of the village and the platoon commander. They had come to protest the killing of one of their children by an American patrol. Lieutenant Caldron had been called in to present his report of the patrol's action. He made his case all right, and since the villagers presented no concrete proof headquarters denied all responsibility for it. The battalion commander attributed the tragedy to VC elements operating in the valley and assured the village elders that the purpose of American patrols was to protect them against such atrocities.

As far as the army was concerned that closed the episode, but I remained greatly troubled and that evening I went again to see the lieutenant.

○

"Now what is it, Glass?"

I got right to the point. "Sir, I request permission to report my conversation with you directly to battalion headquarters."

A tight smile flickered across his face and vanished. "There's no need to do that, Glass."

"I have the need, sir."

"Your conscience still bothers you about that dead gook?"

115

"Yes sir."

"So you want to go over my head?"

"With your permission, sir."

"Don't give me that shit, Glass. If I refused permission you'd go to Colonel Cannon anyway, wouldn't you?"

"Yes sir."

"I'm surprised at you, Glass. Did you really think I'd be so stupid?"

"I don't think you're stupid, sir."

"Well, you're absolutely right about that, Glass. There's nothing for you to tell Colonel Cannon because I've told him everything. Everything! That's how the chain of command operates. Each link strengthens the next one right on up to the top. Fortunately, the villagers didn't see Hammer kill the kid and it all worked out fine. The incident is closed. You understand that, Glass."

"Yes sir. I do now."

"Good. I don't want to regret that I didn't transfer you out of here with Thomas and those other fuckups on that ravine patrol."

His remark surprised me and he saw it in my face.

"You damn well knew Thomas fragged Doll. Everybody in that patrol knew it. But you kept your mouth shut then, didn't you?"

"I didn't witness it."

"Yeah. But it didn't bother you that Doll was killed, did it? You felt he had it coming to him?"

"No sir. That's not how I felt."

"You want to tell me about it?"

"No sir. That incident is closed, too. Isn't it, sir?"

"Yes it is, Glass. Now get your bleeding ass out of here and keep quiet. I don't want to hear any more bitching from you."

"You won't, sir."

O

The next day I was assigned to a night patrol. When we collected in the patrol leader's tent at sunset for the briefing, I was amazed and disturbed to see Hammer there. His friendly greeting, like he was glad to see an old buddy, which I certainly wasn't, increased my uneasiness. Did he know I had gone to see the lieutenant?

During the briefing I had trouble listening to the patrol leader. I was too concerned about Hammer. I didn't believe our being thrown together was an accident. Lieutenant Caldron was too careful to overlook the patrol assignments in his platoon. I kept glancing surreptitiously at Hammer watching for some indication of his attitude but he gave me none. He listened placidly to the patrol leader and seemed unaware of my interest in him. He was a cunning bastard. I had to be more cunning.

O

At that time, the main purpose of our four-man night patrols was to protect the base from enemy infiltration in a hit-and-run attack aimed at blowing up our supplies and ammunition dumps and keeping us under constant harassment. Our patrols, strictly defensive, were heavily armed—rifles, grenades, knives (in case we were overrun) to give us maximum firepower to blast anything we encountered or heard in the dark. It could be particularly unnerving because it was often impossible to distinguish the enemy from our night ambush teams hunting VC in the valley and there had been incidents when we'd shot up our own men in the dark. Mostly, the only indication of trouble was sound—the patter of feet in the underbrush or the snapping of a twig and sometimes the shock of a scream when a man got knifed. The threat of sudden ambush was always there and it worked a terrible strain, demanding intense concentration. You couldn't let your mind wander for a second. The sound you failed to hear could be the last sound in your life.

117

That evening we crawled under the wire and picked our way in the fading light through the minefield surrounding the perimeter of the base. If you didn't go out before total darkness you ran the risk of getting blown apart by one of your own mines. For the same reason night patrols had to return no earlier than dawn, when the light was strong enough to see the way back through the minefield and be seen by the perimeter guards. Moreover, the enemy was more experienced at night fighting and the nature of it put us at an additional disadvantage. The VC took the initiative on their own terrain. They acted. We reacted. Because of these conditions and the higher casualty rate on our side, night patrols were the most worrisome combat duty for the GI.

Once outside the wire and beyond the minefield, we crouched down and proceeded slowly toward a rocky ledge some two hundred meters from the perimeter of the base. We reached it without trouble and proceeded to settle down and listen and watch through the night. The ledge was an excellent observation post overlooking the drop down to the valley from which the enemy had to come. Moreover, it was broad and flat and barren of undergrowth so that no one could approach across it for a distance of thirty meters without being seen.

We sat there in a half-circle, the patrol leader and Hammer side by side facing the valley, the other trooper and myself, our backs to each other, covering the left and right sides of the ledge. For half an hour or more no one spoke as we adjusted to the sounds of the night—the rustle of leaves, the intermittent screech of a bird and the constant hum of mosquitoes that had found us in the darkness. Silently we brushed the air in front of our faces to drive them away. When Hammer slapped the side of his neck, we all tensed up.

"Cut that out," the patrol leader hissed.

"They're eating me alive," Hammer said.

"Let them. You want Charlie killing you alive?"

"Killing me alive. That's good, sarge."

"Knock it off."

The inactivity of that night patrol was more nerve-wracking than a firefight. We just sat there in silence, hour after hour, unable to smoke or move about to ease the stiffness in our legs, constantly straining to distinguish man-made sounds from the natural sounds of the night. After a while the waiting and listening works on your nerves and the flutter of a bird in the dark or the swishing of the grass alarms you. And the night seems endless so that you almost wish the enemy would come simply to release you from the strain of the vigil. But the night passed without incident and in the growing light of the dawn a great sense of relief washed over us. We waited until it was light enough to see clearly before we rose up and prepared to return to the base.

As the mists burned off below us in the valley we could see the fields of elephant grass catching the rays of the early morning sun. We had turned our backs on the view to start back when Hammer called out, "Look!"

The sergeant whirled around. "What is it?"

"There." Hammer pointed down at the tree line bordering the field.

Two black-clad VC armed with AK's were walking slowly along the edge of the field, paralleling the tree line. While we observed them, Hammer raised his M-16 and took aim.

"Hold it," the sergeant said. "They're out of range. You'll only scare them off."

Hammer lowered his rifle. "They'll get away anyway."

"Maybe. Unless they're coming, not going."

"But they're heading south, away from the base."

"Just watch, Hammer. They're going toward the bottom of the trail that leads down from the south end of the base. They could be planning an ambush at the trail. The day patrols go through there."

"Then we got to get them," Hammer said eagerly.

"No. Stay down. We'll report their position. Let the day patrols take care of them."

"Look. What the hell are they doing?" the other trooper said.

"It looks like they're eating," I said.

119

"Yeah," Hammer said. "The dumb fuckers are having a picnic breakfast. Maybe they don't know there's a war on."

"They know. They're not hunting buffalo with those AK's."

"Listen, sarge. If we hustled down the trail we could pick off the fuckers with their mouths full of rice."

"We got to report their location," the sergeant said.

"Sure. Meanwhile, two of us could go down after them."

"Yeah. I'll buy that. I'd like for us to bag them. You know the trail, Hammer?"

"Yeah. I been down it several times."

"What about you, Glass?"

I started to shake my head when Hammer said, "We been out together before, sarge. I'll show him the way."

"Okay. You two go down and stick together. I'll keep a lookout from here." He turned to the other trooper. "Lawton, you hustle your ass back to camp and report their location to the lieutenant and then get back here on the double. I might need you."

"Okay, sarge." Lawton left us and started back to the camp.

Hammer slung his rifle onto his shoulder. "Let's go, Glass."

"Hold it a second," the sergeant said. "If I spot any more of the fuckers I'll fire two short bursts above the trees at the back of the trail so you'll know it's me. It'll mean you're outnumbered and you get your ass back here pronto. I don't want you ambushed. If I'm not here I went back to the base to call in a chopper. We oughta have a fucking radio on these night patrols for something like this."

"Don't worry about us, sarge," Hammer said and he grinned. "I'll bring you back a rice bowl for your souvenir collection."

"Yeah. I ain't got one of those. Now get moving. Those gooks don't eat very much."

We left the sergeant hunched down on the ledge and went into the trees on the right. I knew the trail all right. It was the one we'd taken on the morning of my first patrol to the ravine. But I didn't tell it to Hammer. I wanted him to lead so I could keep him in front of me. I didn't trust him. He'd been much too eager to have me go with him. I had been hoping the sergeant would decide against Hammer's scheme and leave the job to the day patrols but the possibility of trapping two VC out in the open was not something to pass up, particularly when the sergeant had such an enthusiastic volunteer in Hammer. And what could I have said? That I was more worried about my own buddy than the enemy? So there I was, boxed in, alone with Hammer, hunting the enemy but feeling hunted by the man who was leading me down into that valley. I was uncertain of my suspicions; it's easy to get overalarmed in Vietnam. But I knew it couldn't hurt to be cautious.

Halfway down the trail, we stopped for a brief rest. Loaded down by our heavy equipment—rucksacks, flak vests, grenade belts—it had been hard going on the shortcut through the trees, and even on the open trail we were too top-heavy going down the steep incline to keep a strong pace. Hammer had the added burden of his fat, and he paid for it with the sweat that smarted in his eyes and streamed down his face so that he had to keep mopping himself to see where he was going. Every stroke of his sleeve across his face sucked up more of his energy.

When we halted to catch our breath, he was panting like a St. Bernard in summer. "Don't you sweat, Glass?" he said and he popped several salt pills into his mouth and took a large swallow from his canteen.

"Sure." I wiped my face to reassure him.

"You skinny bastards are lucky. You eat like pigs and don't gain an ounce. Me, everything I eat turns to fat."

"Yeah. I guess it's the way you're built."

"You're a smaller target, too. Ever think of that?"

"No. Matter of fact it never occurred to me."

"It should have." He grinned slyly. "Take Charlie. When you get him in your gunsight he don't give you much to shoot at. But me, I must look like a goddamn bull elephant to him."

"I never thought of it that way."

"It evens out though. He can't see so good with those

slit eyes. And I can knock the balls off a buffalo at two hundred meters. Did it once. You shoulda seen that mother jump." He chuckled at the memory and I responded with a smile.

"I guess we better get moving or those fuckers'll be gone."

Hammer pulled at the straps of his rucksack to loosen them. "We should of left this shit with the sarge. We don't need it. Why don't we take off the grenade belts and rucksacks and leave them here? We'd make better time and we can pick them up on the way back."

"We might need the grenades."

"I don't plan to get close enough to use them. I just want a couple of clean shots."

"The grenade belt isn't all that heavy and it makes me feel better. Just in case, you know? And we don't want Charlie finding them if he comes through here. I'd hate getting blown up by one of my own grenades."

"Yeah. I guess you're right." Hammer removed his rucksack and tossed it to the side of the trail. "The gooks can have my fucking C-rations." He waited for me to do the same and I did it to please him. I didn't want him thinking I could carry a bigger load.

As we started again down the trail I lagged so he could lead, but the trail was wide enough for us to walk abreast and he motioned me to catch up.

"What is it?" I asked.

"We better make plans before we get to the bottom."

"What's on your mind?"

"The trail separates into two forks just before the end. It's maybe seven hundred meters from here. It should take us maybe ten more minutes. I'll take the fork to the left and you take the right one to the tree line. If the gooks are still eating we'll just have to sweat them out, and if they've gone past my position by the time I get there you might pick them up. But we might be lucky and catch them smack between us. If that happens, I'll open up on the left and you can hit them from the right and we'll catch them in a cross-fire before they know what hit them. Okay?"

Though Hammer's plan made sense I didn't like the idea of our separating. Instinctively, I resisted. "The sarge told us to stay together."

"Shit, Glass. It's two against two. If they're together and we're separate, it'll confuse them. They'll think they're surrounded and for a change we got the advantage of surprise."

"What if they split up and cover both forks?"

"Then it's one on one and they ain't expecting us. They'll be watching the trail and we'll be in the cover of the trees. Either way we got the break."

I still felt uneasy but I had run out of objections. "Okay," I said finally.

After that we were silent and our pace increased down the trail. When we reached the fork, we stopped before separating to study the terrain. We could see ahead through the trees to the field below. It looked so serene in the early morning sunshine that I found it hard to believe it might become the scene of a firefight.

"I don't think they came through yet," Hammer said. "Good luck, Glass." He grinned at me and started into the trees on the left.

I remained rooted at the fork. I hoped the VC had finished their breakfast and were long gone. I had no stomach for killing. I was a misfit in an alien world that was closing in on me and I felt hopeless to do anything about it. I trembled with fear and anger. My anger focused on Lieutenant Caldron. I was convinced he had schemed to get rid of me. It seemed like a long time before I was finally able to leave the trail and proceed into the trees along the right fork. I had gone some forty meters through the undergrowth when I reached the line of trees bordering the field. I picked a position in the shadows that gave me a clear view of the field and the entrance to the right fork of the trail and I waited. It was all very quiet and peaceful. I watched. I saw nothing in the landscape. I raised my rifle and squinting through the gunsight I swept the barrel slowly across the field. It narrowed my line of vision and gave me a pinpoint view. In the gunsight, the field sharpened into separate blades of grass swaying and parting in the warm wind.

There was nothing else until my sight crossed the line of trees on my left and I caught a reflection of light in the dark foliage. I steadied my aim on it. It was a gun barrel glinting in the sunlight, pointing like a finger at the open field. It took me a second to realize it was Hammer's rifle surveying the field as mine was. With a sense of relief I lowered my rifle and fixed my gaze on the glint of the gun barrel. It told me exactly where Hammer was. Now there was nothing to do but wait. Though I tried to concentrate on the field, I kept glancing back toward the gun barrel, pointing steadily ahead. After several minutes I began to wonder why Hammer kept such a constant vigil with his rifle. And then I saw the reason.

Thirty meters directly out from his position, two heads bobbed just above the tips of the grass. They were moving south parallel to the tree line. Hammer must have spotted them coming from his left and he was patiently tracking them. I raised my rifle and found them in my sight. They were VC all right. Their rifles were slung and tilting as they moved through the grass. They were passing Hammer's position and were about two hundred meters from me and approaching at a slow pace, looking ahead, unaware of the danger threatening them from the tree line. I gripped the trigger and waited expecting Hammer to open up. He had them in close range, forty meters, but with each step they were moving away from him and coming toward me on a line thirty meters out from my position. I didn't understand why Hammer held his fire. He had the clean shots he had hoped for. As they came on, I felt the muscles constricting in my chest. My arms trembled. Sweat ran into my eyes and I blinked to clear my vision and concentrated hard to steady my rifle. The VC were on my left at a fifty-degree angle and nearing the apex of a triangle between Hammer's position and mine when I realized Hammer was waiting for the perfect point of the crossfire. In the moment when I estimated the VC had reached the apex of the triangle, I sucked in my breath and steadied my aim on the first of the two bobbing heads and listened for the crack of Hammer's rifle.

Seconds passed and then it came. Two shots in rapid succession. In the instant of the second shot, the head in my sight turned sharply to the left and disappeared as I pumped several rounds before releasing the trigger. I raised my eyes over the gunsight. In the spot where the two VC had been the grasses shimmered in the bright sunlight. Nothing else stirred. I didn't know if Hammer's shots had killed the VC or only wounded them or missed them entirely. In the limited view of my gunsight I only knew my target head had disappeared before I had gotten off my first round.

I stayed in my position and waited, my gaze wandering from the field to the spot on the tree line where I had seen Hammer's rifle. It was gone and I could see no sign of him in the shadows of the trees. Where was he? We had made no plan for joining up again. I thought of backtracking through the trees to his position but I decided against it. Let him find me. He knew my location from my gunfire. Then, unexpectedly, Hammer appeared out of the shadows of the tree line and stood at the edge of the field, holding his rifle up and signaling in my direction. He surprised me. I didn't expect him to expose himself to the open field. He had to be certain he had killed the VC. Was he that certain of his marksmanship? Two shots. Two heads. I wasn't that sure. Still, the sight of Hammer waving his rifle in my direction made me feel I was being overcautious. Hammer wasn't one to take a stupid chance. He didn't go into hootches alone.

I stepped out from my cover into the bright sun and waved toward him. He motioned to me to join him. Picking my way carefully through the clumps of grass, I took two or three steps when the shot rang out. I never saw it fired. The bullet had whined past the left side of my head and the next thing I knew I was lying face down in the grass. It was a moment before I felt a warm trickle in my ear and realized it was blood. The bullet must have grazed me though I felt no pain. Instinctively, I didn't move or make a sound. The blood filling my ear was uncomfortable but I resisted clearing it. I held my breath and listened. Not a sound. I raised my head slightly but I could see nothing except the grass blowing gently. I knew the shot had to have been fired from the tree line to graze the left side of my head. I must have been looking down at the moment Hammer fired. He had been at least a hundred meters from me and the thought that he was out there, stalking me, tightened every muscle in my body. I was afraid to move. My rifle was under me, clenched in my fingers. I had to free it before he got any closer. Thank God it was on automatic. I rolled slowly on my right side and inched my rifle along the ground up to my chest and lay still. My only chance was to play dead and wait for him. He had to make certain he had gotten me. It seemed like an eternity before I heard the ominous sound of footsteps cracking the dry grass and then Hammer's voice calling my name. The cunning fool. I estimated he was twenty meters away when the footsteps stopped. The silence was immense as we both listened for the sound of the other. I was afraid to breathe. Finally the grass crackled again and the footsteps grew louder. Ten meters away, I saw him. He was standing still again, the middle of his torso framed by the grass and the edge of my helmet. The barrel of his rifle pointed down between his legs. After a moment, he came on again, the grenades bouncing on the belt across his belly. He never got the chance to raise his rifle. I bolted up and fired at his middle. The burst exploded the grenades and threw him backward several feet into the grass. I jumped to my feet and stood over him. He was lying on his back. The grenades had ripped open his belly and chest and some of his guts splotched his face. I turned away. My legs trembled and I dropped to my knees and vomited. I felt a wave of exhilaration to be alive and an excitement at having out-witted Hammer. Happily, I vomited again, releasing the tension in my gut. The fresh air was sweet and I sucked it deep into my lungs.

○

On my way back up the trail I planned the report I would give of the action. The details were worked out easily and the bullet that had nicked me made the case perfect.

The blood had caked in my ear and dried in trickles down the side of my face. It didn't bother me and I purposely didn't clean myself.

Halfway along the trail, two short bursts of gunfire sounded overhead in the trees behind me. It was the patrol leader's warning that there were more VC down in the valley. But it didn't matter now. It was too late to concern me—or Hammer.

○

The patrol leader and the other trooper, Lawton, were on the ledge observing the valley when I came on them through the trees. They turned abruptly at the sound of my footsteps and then lowered their rifles. "What happened?" the patrol leader asked. He pointed at the bloody side of my face. "You okay?"

"Yeah. It's just the tip of my ear."

"What happened?"

I told him the story briefly, sticking to the facts up to the point we had caught the VC in our crossfire.

"I heard your fire," the sergeant said. "But then it got quiet and then there was another burst. Did you get them?"

"Yeah. But they got Hammer. We thought we killed them in the crossfire. That's when it got quiet and Hammer went into the field to check. I came out of my position and we were closing in when one of the gooks fired at him and then clipped me before I blasted him. He was awful fast with that AK. I got him with half my clip."

"You were lucky."

"Yeah."

"You sure Hammer's dead?"

"Yeah. The gook exploded his grenade belt. Blew him wide open."

"Jesus! Poor bastard," the sergeant said.

"At least we got two for one," Lawton said.

"You got shit," the sergeant said. "Hammer was a good man, worth ten gooks."

"At least," I said.

127

After glancing down at the valley, the sergeant turned away. "We better be getting back. I spotted five more VC going south. A gunship could still pick them up. You hear my warning shots, Glass? You had me worried."

"Yeah. I was halfway back by then."

"You sure were lucky. Poor Hammer, blown up by his own grenades. That's a tough way to get it."

"It sure is," I said.

"How's your ear?" the sergeant said.

"It doesn't bother me. I guess it looks worse than it is."

"It don't look bad. Charlie just got a little piece of it. The medics'll clean you up. You got to watch out it don't get infected. I knew a guy got a scratch from one of them fucking vines. It looked like nothing but it ate away half his face. They hadda send him home."

"This was from an AK round," I said. "I wouldn't mind if they sent me home."

"Yeah." The sergeant grinned.

"You got a Purple Heart coming," Lawton said.

"That's just what I need."

"Move your stupid ass, Lawton," the sergeant said. "We ain't got all day."

○

At the base, a medic washed out my ear and cauterized the wound and marked "fit for duty" on my medical report.

"You want a Purple Heart for this?" the medic asked, without looking up from the form, "or you want to wait until you get something juicier?"

"Put me in," I said. "I want it for a souvenir. I'll make up a juicy story to go with it."

"Yeah. I bet you will. Okay, Glass, that's all. If the ear gets infected bring it back and we'll cut it off."

"Fuck you."

○

At noon, I was getting ready to go to mess when the sergeant came into my tent.

"The lieutenant wants to see you after chow."

128

"What for?"

"I dunno."

"You told him everything, didn't you?"

"Sure. He was pretty hot about what we found. Sent out *two* gunships after the other gooks."

"He say anything about Hammer?"

"Yeah. He felt real bad about that. Said Hammer was one of the best. He's having one of the choppers pick him up. I told him near the bottom of the trail, right?"

"Right. But there isn't much to ship home."

"You'd be surprised what the medics can do long as the face is okay. I seen them close up a guy from his balls to his Adam's apple. He'd been ripped open by a mine. I mean gutted like a fish. They stuffed it all back in and sewed him up and when they decked him out in a clean uniform he looked good as new. His family could have left the coffin open at the wake. It's the face they can't do nothing with."

"Hammer's face was okay," I said.

"That's somethin'. Last year a buddy of mine caught a mortar round full in the face. Tore out the whole left side of his head. They shipped him sealed with his dog tags and warned the family not to open the casket. His old man wouldn't believe he was inside less he saw for himself. Said the army could make a mistake. Said he wasn't going to bury no stranger with his boy's dog tags. He made them open the box. He must of recognized half the face cause he keeled over dead right there. Heart attack. Knocked the coffin on the floor right at the wake with everybody watching. What a mess. The stubborn bastard."

"How'd you find out?"

"His sister wrote me the whole story and a good thing. You don't think about things like that in case you get it. Know what I mean? I wrote my old man about it. Told him not to open it if they ever shipped me home in a sealed box. Just bury it, I told him."

"I never thought about it," I said.

"That's what I mean. You gotta think about something like that. Not that my old man would have heart failure. He's a tough old bastard. But my mother's something else. I

129

wouldn't want her to see me like that. I mean if it happened, I'd like to make it easy on her."

"Yeah. No sense in her suffering."

"Exactly my feelings. Say, how's your ear?" He stared at it. "You can't hardly tell nothing if you don't look too close. They cleaned it up good."

"It's okay. I don't even know it's there unless I touch it."

"It looked real bad when I first saw the blood. You sure were lucky. A couple of more inches over and we'da been shipping you home, too."

"In a closed box, huh?"

The sergeant laughed. "You're real cool, Glass. You're okay. How about some chow, buddy? We missed out on breakfast."

"Yeah."

"I hate them night patrols, just sitting out there waiting for Charlie. No food, no grass, and when something happens like this morning you get screwed out of breakfast. I hate missing my eggs and bacon. It's the only fucking good meal of the day."

"That's the way I feel."

We left the tent and headed for the mess. I wasn't looking forward to another combat session with the lieutenant but it didn't worry me. I had no complaints this time. I was beyond that now. I wasn't bucking the system anymore and in a strange way I felt good about it. Maybe it was the sergeant's morbid stories that had something to do with my new sense of myself. His obsessive interest in the gruesome details of death amused me but it also had another effect. It made me aware that I was less worried about dying because I had no one who cared about me—no one to mourn me. If I were shipped home in a sealed coffin no one at the orphanage would be the least interested in opening the lid to be sure of my identity.

And even now as I write this I am not preoccupied with death. The court may decide to take my life for what I have done. So be it. But it will never know where my head is at. That is only for you to judge.

130

○

The lieutenant sat stiffly in his chair and rolled a pencil nervously between his fingers. This time I was relaxed and he got straight to the point.

"The sergeant told me what happened, Glass. But I need the full details for my report. We've got an obligation to tell the family all we know about Hammer's death."

"I understand, sir."

"Why don't you just tell me exactly what happened after you spotted the VC."

"Right."

Calmly, I recited the action in greater detail than I'd told it to the patrol sergeant. While I talked the lieutenant made a diagram and notes on a pad, and when I finished he launched into his cross-examination.

"There's one thing I don't understand, Glass. If you and Hammer were a hundred meters apart when you had the gooks in the crossfire, why'd you come together before you went out in the field after them? Why didn't you move in keeping them in the crossfire?"

I shrugged. "When Hammer showed himself and motioned to me to join him, I figured he knew he nailed them. In fact, he said so when I came up to him."

"Did you think they were dead?"

"I wasn't sure. Like I said, when Hammer opened fire the gook I was aiming at dropped as I fired. I didn't know if Hammer'd hit him or I'd hit him or he just hit the dirt. You know how fast it happens."

"But Hammer *was* sure?"

"That's what he said."

"He's a helluva marksman."

"Yeah."

"If he was so sure the gooks were dead, why'd you go into the field?"

"Hammer wanted to get their AK's."

131

"And how far apart were you and Hammer as you walked into the field?"

"Three, four meters."

"Side by side?"

"No. Hammer was first. I was a little behind him and to the right."

"Like this?" He made two small circles on the pad and pushed it across the desk to me.

"About like that," I said.

"And then what happened?"

"I told you, sir."

"Tell me again."

"The gook opened up and blasted us."

"Us?"

"He caught Hammer across the middle and clipped my ear before I got him." I touched the tip of my ear.

"Yeah. I just got the medical report. It's just a superficial flesh wound. You were real lucky, Glass. Hammer gets bagged by his own grenades and you walk away from it. It's hard to believe." He looked directly at me and his eyes narrowed to slits. "I'm leveling with you, Glass. I can't picture Hammer risking his ass that way. He must have been damn sure those gooks were dead."

"He had me convinced. I didn't want to go into the field."

"Yeah. Did you get the AK's?"

"No sir. I got out fast."

"Then how do you know you got the gook?"

"He didn't do any more firing. It was awful quiet after I gave him my clip. I know I got him."

"I sent a chopper to pick up Hammer. The medics'll have to go over him carefully before we ship the body."

His implication was clear and I was greatly tempted to tell him how lucky I really was, that they would find only the grenade shrapnel and not the M-16 bullets that had exploded them.

"He's in awful shape," I said. "The grenades ripped him

open. I could hardly look at him. But I guess the medics are used to that. They've seen everything. And I hear they do a good patch job as long as the face is okay."

"You're a real cool cat, Glass."

"Sir?"

"I know you had it in for Hammer. Why don't you say it, Glass? You're glad he got it."

"No sir. I'm just glad it wasn't me. That's only natural." Nervously, I pushed the pad back across the desk to him. Though he had no case against me, he made me uneasy. I was convinced he had assigned me to the night patrol expecting a wholly different outcome. I was growing furious with his baiting tactics and my hostility came out.

"Why did you assign me and Hammer to the same patrol after you said you wouldn't?"

My question startled him but he quickly recovered. "The platoon sergeant made up the roster. It was just a routine night patrol to protect the perimeter."

"But you see every roster, don't you, sir?"

"Yes." He kept his eyes fixed on me. "I didn't think anything of it. The other business was settled. Hammer came out of it clean. He didn't have any beef against you, did he?"

He watched me eagerly and I was beginning to regret having opened the subject, but I persisted. "Did Hammer know I'd been in to see you about that other situation?"

"What are you getting at, Glass? What's eating you? You can level with me." He faked a smile.

"Nothing. Nothing at all, sir. I was just surprised to see Hammer last night after what you told me."

"Did he say anything to you about that other episode?"

"No sir. Actually he was pretty friendly."

"But you were suspicious of him. Is that it?"

"No sir. Just surprised, like I said."

"Tell me, Glass. Whose idea was it to go out after the gooks?"

"Hammer's idea. He was real eager. He convinced the patrol leader."

133

"How come Lawton didn't go with him?"

I met the lieutenant's searching gaze. "Hammer wanted me. The sergeant had no objection."

"That must have worried you, being alone with Hammer if you thought he knew you'd ratted on him."

"Yeah. I thought about it. It made me extra cautious."

"And you decided you had to get him before he got you. Isn't that right?"

It was all hanging out now and I rammed it home.

"Charlie got Hammer, lieutenant, and he clipped me. I didn't shoot my own ear with an M-16. It's too tricky."

A red flush washed over the lieutenant's face. "You're an arrogant bastard, Glass. A goddamn misfit. And I'm going to get your ass. Now get the hell out of here."

His fury surprised me. I hadn't expected him to blow off. But I was pleased. Now I knew where I stood, not that I could do much about it. I got to my feet, saluted indifferently at the top of his head and left him staring solemnly at the notes on his pad. He had a lot to think about and so did I.

I was a misfit all right but I relished my small victory. It didn't last long, though. The lieutenant's frustration worried me. He could send me out with another Hammer. Ultimately, he would find a way to get rid of me. What could I do about it?

That night, smoking grass to ease my tension, I played with the thought of rolling a live grenade into the lieutenant's tent while he slept. Why not? It was not an uncommon practice. I slept on it and I slept soundly.

○

The next morning the bulletin board listed two items of special interest to me:

Private Richard Hammer, KIA, is recommended posthumously for the Bronze Star for volunteering to destroy an enemy ambush, which he accomplished at the cost of his life.

Private David Glass is to report to the day ser-

134

geant, platoon headquarters, for his transfer orders to Camp Jordan, Third Cavalry Division (Airmobile) at Long Hoa.

Lieutenant Caldron's decision to transfer me came as a surprise and a relief. I thought it a happy solution for both of us. Perhaps he had suspected my potheaded thoughts.

When the day sergeant handed me my travel orders, he said, "You ship out this afternoon, Glass. When you get to Camp Jordan you'll be reassigned to a gunship as a door gunner. It's nice, clean work. No more slogging in the boondocks. You're a lucky shit, Glass."

"Yeah."

"Say, weren't you on that patrol with Hammer yesterday?"

"Yeah."

"How come he gets put in for a Star and you don't?"

I shrugged. "He was KIA. I only got a flesh wound."

"Yeah," the sergeant snorted. "I know what you mean. The only heroes in this outfit are the dead ones."

7.

In all the time I spent at Camp Jordan I never got used to the misery of the heat. Situated on land fill at the top of the Mekong Delta at Long Hoa, the camp seemed to suck up the wet heat from the surrounding rice paddies like a wet sponge. Except for the time spent in the air on missions, I lived in a constant state of sweat. And it never cooled off at night as it did on the plateau at Cam Binh. After a day's action I had always counted on a good night's sleep to get myself together for the next day's patrol. Now I slept fitfully, bathed in my own sweat, and often awoke more exhausted than when I'd gone to sleep.

But most everything else at Camp Jordan was an improvement over Cam Binh. I had escaped the tyranny of Lieutenant Caldron, and door gunner on a gunship was cleaner and far less torturous work than hacking through swamp and jungle on foot patrols. And it better suited my nature. I found flying exhilarating and, with the enemy remote and unseen, firefights were impersonal from the air. On those early missions I fired my machine gun at targets of terrain—trees, jungle, ravines—not at men or women or children.

Of course, there were supposed to be enemy soldiers at the exploding end of our rocket and machine-gun fire but if you didn't actually see them it made a difference in your head. And for two weeks, until I went out on an evacuation mission, I saw no mutilated dead or agonized wounded on either side. It was a relief while it lasted.

○

That day our mission was a special one. A large-scale firefight had raged all morning against a strong contingent of VC outside the village of Loi Cu. By early afternoon, when the action broke off, our troops had killed a dozen of the enemy and taken some prisoners. The colonel leading our forces had radioed for an armed chopper to take out the captured for interrogation and processing. Sergeant Bright, our chopper pilot, had briefed us on our way to the landing zone.

After we set down on a grassy knoll in the middle of the rice paddy about two hundred meters from where we had spotted our forces, Sergeant Bright told me to report to the colonel and tell him we were ready to lift off as soon as we were loaded.

"Better take your M-16," he said. "You never know what's still out there."

I slogged through the wet fields and came on the colonel and a lieutenant and several troopers standing guard over the prisoners. There were six of them—two men, two women and two very young children. The kids, a boy and a girl, clung to their mothers and the entire group looked very frightened. I told the colonel we were ready to load the prisoners. He made a point of correcting me. He said they were "detainees" until they were found otherwise after interrogation by Intelligence. I was astounded by the colonel's strict interpretation of the code, especially since he had just been through a bloody firefight. Looking at the group huddled on the ground, I wondered how Intelligence determined if four-year-old children were detainees or war

137

prisoners. Were they interrogated or simply judged by their association with their mothers?

The colonel assigned the lieutenant and two corporals to help me take the detainees to the landing zone and get them out fast. He was concerned about the VC force that had retreated into the tree line a thousand meters south across the paddy. He thought they were holed up there with additional forces. Uncertain of their strength and deployment, he was waiting for reinforcements before pursuing them. He told me to be certain the chopper stayed well clear of the tree line after lift-off. I appreciated the warning. Even at a distance of several hundred meters, a single AK round striking a vital part of the rotors or tearing through the gearbox can bring down a chopper like a rock.

When the colonel ordered us to get moving, the two corporals were quick to jab at the frightened detainees with their rifle butts to get them on their feet. The two women, each clutching a child, rose quickly, but the two men were hesitant and the rifle butts slammed harder into their backs. They jumped up then and cowered close to the women for protection. One of the troopers started to push them forward using his rifle as a bar against their backs. The other trooper cursed at them and punched at the woman closest to him. Hunching her shoulders against the blows, the woman carrying the boy stumbled forward, lost her footing, and fell to the ground with the child under her. The boy shrieked with fright and she quickly stood up and held him more tightly.

As the group moved off, the colonel shouted at the troopers, "Take it easy. Don't beat on them."

They let up and we headed back across the muddy fields toward the chopper. With the troopers prodding the group and the lieutenant and me following, we marched along the rise that separated the gullies planted with young rice shoots. After we had gone about thirty meters, one of the troopers glanced back for a moment and then began again to jab at the captives with his rifle barrel. From the opposite side, the other trooper did the same. Each time they struck, the captives stumbled and slipped in the mud trying to avoid the blows at their arms and legs. Cursing and laughing, the troopers continued to take turns at striking the captives. I looked expectantly at the lieutenant, but he too was amused at their game and he grinned at me. Finally, after one of the women fell in the mud with her child and they kicked her until she scrambled back on her feet, I protested to the lieutenant: "There's no reason to keep hitting them and it's only slowing us up."

"What's your big hurry?" the lieutenant said. "We got a bellyful from these ginks all morning and the boys are just letting off some steam. It's good for them. For me, too. If it wasn't for the colonel's holy goddamn attitude, I'da had them all shot back there when we caught them."

"Even if they're just villagers working these rice fields?" I said.

"What the hell do you know about it? The first gunfire this morning came from that village just north. We were moving in peaceably when all hell hit us at the edge of the paddy. Maybe there was a hundred of them to twenty of us. It took four hours before they lost enough gooks to break it off and run for the woods. We found this bunch hiding right in the middle of their dead. The squawling kids gave them away. They're VC, flyboy. The whole fucking country is VC for my money."

The kids too? I wanted to ask. But I knew enough to shut up. The lieutenant and the two troopers regarded me with hostility. We walked on in silence. Then one of the troopers viciously punched his rifle into the groin of one of the men who had slowed behind the others. The man let out a howl and dropped to his knees, clutching his genitals. The other captives halted and turned to look at him. The man remained on his knees, head bowed, moaning and swaying with pain.

"Get him up," the lieutenant said.

The trooper's thick boot lashed out and caught the man

139

full against the side of his jaw. He toppled sideways into the gully and lay there in the mud, his eyes staring in fright at the trooper standing over him. "Get up, you gink!"

Shaking his head, the man covered it with his hands. The boot smashed into his ribs. "Get up!"

Expecting another blow, the man doubled his body into the smallest possible target. Both women were shrieking now and shielding the heads of their crying children. The other man started to move toward the man on the ground. The second trooper stepped in front of him and jammed the stock of his rifle into the man's chest, knocking him backward against the women.

I slung my rifle onto my shoulder and went toward the fallen man.

"What the hell are you doing?" the lieutenant said.

"I'll get him up. Beating on him won't do it."

"You stay out of it, flyboy. He's going to get up all by himself." The lieutenant pointed at the group. "Wade, you keep them moving to the chopper. We'll follow with this one."

Wade pushed and cursed at the captives and got them moving again. I stayed back with the lieutenant. We had only gone about a hundred and fifty meters and were still that distance again from the landing zone where the chopper sat, its rotors idling in a steady hum. I knew my pilot was eager to take off and it made me anxious. The chopper was a sitting duck in the flat, open paddy. My impulse was to raise the fallen man to his feet and get him moving. I looked at Wade hustling the others away and told the lieutenant we'd better catch up.

"Don't worry about it, flyboy. Your chopper won't take off without you." He looked at the trembling captive, bunched up in a ball. "Kick his ass, Hawley. If he doesn't get up in two seconds, shoot the bastard."

Hawley's boot thudded into the man's backside at the base of his spine. The man screamed from the blow but remained still except for his hands covering his head. They were shaking as if he had lost control of them. Hawley

140

kicked at him again and again. With each blow, the man shuddered and then tightened into himself.

"You'll break his back," I said.

"Shoot him," the lieutenant said.

"Sir?"

"Shoot him!"

Hawley clicked a round into the chamber, swung his rifle inches above the man's head and fired. The bullet shredded the man's hand and split open the whole side of his head. Hawley's boots were splattered with bloody pulp. He wiped them against the dead man's pajamas.

"You keep your mouth shut about this, flyboy," the lieutenant said. "Let's move it."

The lieutenant and Hawley started after the others. I followed behind them. After a few steps I glanced back toward the village, wondering if the colonel and his men had been roused by the shot. I could see nothing but the high grass bordering the village. I realized it was foolish to think a single rifle shot would arouse the attention of anyone in this land of incessant gunfire.

When we caught up with the others, the lieutenant said, "It's okay, Wade. The gink resisted and we shot him."

"Yeah," Wade said. "What about this bunch? I can't take much more of them bawling kids."

"Keep them moving out to that chopper."

The children were crying without letup. The man and the two women stared at us, their eyes full of fright. They knew what had happened, and when Wade and Hawley barked at them to march they quickened their pace—eager to get to the safety of the chopper.

We were less than a hundred meters from the chopper when automatic gunfire opened up from the tree line to the south. It was sporadic at first and inaccurate at that range— a thousand meters—but we hit the ground, leaving our captives standing, bewildered, suddenly cut off from our attention. They clustered together trying to shield one another. Bullets whined through the still air. I yelled at them to get down but they remained on their feet. The women shrieked and clenched their children more tightly and the kids wailed more loudly. Beside me, the lieutenant and the two troopers were firing blindly at the tree line though it was beyond effective range of their weapons.

The whole scene of those wailing women with their screaming children standing alone in the midst of that gunfire enraged me because I was impotent to do anything about it. Finally, the lieutenant and the troopers stopped firing and it was then I heard the rotors of the chopper revving up to full power. My impulse was to get up from that gully and make a run for it. I didn't want to be left behind. That was my gunship. I belonged with it. But those captives kept me from running. I couldn't abandon them. I had to get them out safely. They were my responsibility. I thought of the poor bastard lying dead in the gully with his head blown apart. He was no longer a detainee. He was a dead enemy statistic now. I yelled at the women and motioned to them to get down. This time they responded, squatting on the ground in a tight huddle.

Right then, the first mortar rounds started dropping in off on our right, exploding dully in the soft mud and vomiting up clumps of earth and green shoots of rice.

"What do we do now?" Hawley asked the lieutenant.

"I'm for getting out of here before they zero in," Wade said.

"Yeah," the lieutenant agreed. "We haven't got the firepower." He rammed a fresh clip into his rifle. "We're going back, flyboy. You better hustle your ass out to that chopper. It's not going to sit there long with these mortars popping."

"What about the captives?" I asked.

"We'll take care of them."

"I'm supposed to take them out. The colonel gave me orders."

"Don't worry about the colonel. I'll handle it."

I didn't know what to do. With the mortars coming in I knew Sergeant Bright couldn't wait much longer. He'd have to lift off. With every second he was risking getting boxed in.

"We can still get them to the chopper. The mortars haven't got our range," I said.

"The gooks in the tree line would like that," Wade snapped. "They're just waiting for us to make a run for it so they can light us all up. I ain't going near that chopper, lieutenant. Why are we risking our ass for a bunch of fucking ginks? It don't make no sense, lieutenant."

The lieutenant stared at me. "This is as far as we go, flyboy. Start moving. That's an order."

"I'll take them with me," I said.

"You'll take nothing. You don't move now and I guarantee you'll never get to that chopper. You understand?"

I looked at the grim faces of the lieutenant and Wade and Hawley and then I was on my feet and running with my head down past the captives. I couldn't look at them. I had gone fifteen, twenty meters, pumping my legs hard over the rise between the gullies, heading straight for the chopper, when the automatic rifle fire rattled behind me. I didn't look back. The screams told me everything. My chest felt like a hot coal was growing inside and I couldn't suck enough air into my lungs but I managed to keep my footing and keep pumping. There was a second burst of gunfire and the screaming stopped and there was only the sound of the mortars exploding and the whir of the rotors again in my ears. Fifty meters from the chopper I began to feel safe. They weren't going to shoot me. My crew could see me by now and I knew the chopper would wait. I kept up the pace until I was under the rotors with the wind blasting at me. It knocked me down. Above the din of the rotors I heard voices yelling my name. I struggled up and grasped the doorframe. Jonesy, the other door gunner, pulled me aboard. I fell on the deck panting as the chopper lifted off and moved low over the ground.

"You okay?" Jonesy shouted.

I nodded and sat up, sucking air into my mouth. He left me and went to his position behind his machine gun. We were moving fast over the ground now, away from the tree line, and rising up sharply to gain quick altitude so that if we were hit critically the pilot would have enough height and the time to try a forced landing. Another few seconds and we were at a thousand feet and leveling off, crossing

143

over the village north of the paddy—well beyond the range of the mortars. Unslinging my rifle, I put it aside and took my place at my door gun.

By the time I had adjusted my headset, Sergeant Bright's voice came over the intercom. "You there, Glass?"

"I'm here."

"What the hell happened back there?"

"We were coming with the captives when Charlie opened up."

"Where the hell are the prisoners?"

"I had to leave them. The lieutenant ordered me to get out without them."

"We sure sweated you out, Glass. Another minute and I was going to have to leave you back there."

"Yeah. I sweated some myself when I heard you revving up."

"What're they going to do with the prisoners?"

"The lieutenant didn't say." I hesitated and then asked: "Didn't you see us coming?"

"We didn't see nothing but the fire coming from that tree line. How many were you?"

"The lieutenant and two troopers and the prisoners."

"Poor bastards. I hope they get their asses out of there."

"Yeah."

We were flying a wide circle pattern above the village that took us over the north end of the rice paddy. It was laid out in a near perfect square. As we came around the second time, I could see the cluster of troops in the north-west corner close to the edge of the village. Southwest of them, near the spot where I'd left the lieutenant and the troopers, mortar shells exploded in quick, small flashes of fire. My eyes searched the paddy but I couldn't see anything moving.

As we wheeled in a left arc taking us back over the village, Sergeant Bright came on again: "Glass, I think your buddies might be pinned down in that mortar fire. Without our cargo, we can go home but we might make a nice, low pass on that tree line and give Charlie some rocket fire. The

144

boys down there might appreciate it. What do you think?"

"It's okay with me, sarge," I said. "But hold it straight over the trees, west to east, so they can't see us coming."

"Right. I'll make a wide pattern and come in at treetop level. You and Jonesy point them guns straight down and pour it on. We'll give them our whole load. You got that, Jonesy?"

"Got it, sarge."

"Good. Here we go."

We circled wide north of the village and then started dropping down fast as we came across it. We were at three hundred feet and still dropping when we scooted over the troops in the northeast pocket of the paddy. They looked up and waved with their rifles, the barrels flashing in the sun. From my position at the left door gun, the whole square of the paddy stretched below me. I gazed across the field and spotted the landing zone. Just beyond it, moving east away from the pocket of troops, I saw them—three troopers. Cut off from the main body of troops by the mortars exploding south and west of them, they were heading north toward the protection of a field of elephant grass. Suddenly, they dropped to the ground and I lost sight of them. I fixed the spot in my mind.

We were running a course along the western side of the paddy and the sun on our right cast the shadow of the chopper on a line marking the edge of the rice field. We were up a hundred feet and still coming down as we approached the western end of the tree line. The ship shuddered as Sergeant Bright cut the power to make the tight turn over the trees and then it sprang forward again under full power. We were leveled off ten feet above the treetops. The VC were positioned eight hundred meters dead ahead. Seconds after we completed the turn, the co-pilot fired off the first two rockets, then two more and two more. The gunship staggered through the air. The carpet of leaves flashed under us. I set the machine gun on automatic and flipped the barrel straight down and gripped the trigger. One, two, three, four, five seconds. I squeezed the

145

trigger with my right hand and used my left to feed the belt. Jonesy opened up on the other side. The ship sprang forward, rattling and shaking. I watched the belt until it was half eaten and then I released the trigger. I had plans for the rest of it. Jonesy kept firing until he was out. By that time, we had run the tree line and started into the turn north. I swung my gun level and gripped the trigger again.

"Man, we powdered them," Sergeant Bright said. "Let's see how the boys liked it."

He wheeled the chopper straight up the east line of the paddy and stayed low.

Good, I thought.

"I'll hold it until we hit the top of the field and then I'll cut back across to the troops near the village. Let me know what you see down there."

"I can't see the paddy from my side," Jonesy said.

Perfect, I thought.

"I can see the whole field, sarge," I said. "The mortars have stopped.

"You bet your ass."

I shut out the conversation on the intercom and concentrated my gaze on the paddy field. I picked out the rise of the landing zone ahead on my right. We were coming up on it fast when I saw the three troopers again. They were moving toward the high grass in the northeast corner of the paddy. I swung the gun around and got them in the gunsight. I tracked them, turning the barrel as the chopper banked into a wide turn directly over the field of elephant grass. The lieutenant and the two troopers were nearing the edge of the field. They were no more than two hundred meters from the end of my gun. As we came out of the turn ahead of them, they didn't look up. I held the gunsight on them and fired, getting off ten, twelve rounds before releasing the trigger. All three toppled forward and disappeared in the elephant grass.

With the cool wind blowing at my face, a heavy sweat broke out all over my body. It was done but I had no time to think about it.

"What were you firing at, Glass?"

I hesitated and then said quickly, "I spotted some VC in the paddy, sarge."

"Maybe it was them prisoners. They coulda got away during the shelling."

"Could be."

"Did you get them?"

"Yeah. I got them."

"Hey, look down there," Sergeant Bright said excitedly. "They're cheering us."

We were passing over the edge of the village. Below on our left, the pocket of troopers were waving up at us with their rifles and helmets. There was no firing from the tree line.

"We sure gave them a big boost."

In response to the cheers, Sergeant Bright took the chopper down to a hundred feet and made a final pass, banking the ship from side to side, until we were well past the troopers and flying low over the flat lush green landscape of the Delta crisscrossed by the brown ribbons of water that fed the rice fields. A village of thatched huts appeared up ahead and the sergeant went into a long steady climb up to two thousand feet before he leveled off and turned north toward home.

For several minutes we flew in silence and then Sergeant Bright came on the intercom:

"Glass."

"Here, sarge."

"Something just struck me funny."

"What's that?"

"We came here to pick up them prisoners and maybe we ended up shooting them."

"Yeah."

"Funny the way things work out, ain't it?"

"Sure is."

Jonesy broke in excitedly. "We really smeared them. Them rockets went right in on Charlie's head. He heard us coming but he couldn't see us. Must've scared the piss out of him. That's the way I like it, sarge. Everything going out and nothing coming back."

147

The conversation rattled on all the way back to the base but I dropped out of it and they didn't miss me. It was the usual post-mission talk and I wasn't up to it.

○

Going into the base we passed two transport choppers going out. They were fully loaded with troops—the reinforcements the colonel had asked for, I figured. It would be a mop-up operation for them now.

On the way to the operations shack, Sergeant Bright asked me how many of the enemy I got in the rice paddy. I told him there were four. I said nothing about the two kids.

"Was that all of them?"

"Yeah. Why?"

"The body count, man. That's the first thing they ask— what's the kill. You know that."

"Yeah. I wasn't thinking."

"Something bugging you, Glass? You look bad."

"Nothing. I'm just tired. I didn't sleep so good last night."

"Why don't you hit the sack. We don't have nothing on till tomorrow. I'll take care of the debriefing for you."

"Thanks."

I left them at the operations shack and went back to my bunk. It was almost time for evening chow but I decided to skip it. I had no appetite.

○

Last week, sitting on my prison cot and writing what you have just read, I found it difficult to go on. I was blocked in trying to recapture the feelings I had that night at Camp Jordan after I left the others at the operations shack. Though that day was a most significant one in my year in Vietnam, so much has happened to me since then that I was hard put to find that night in my memory. But, of course, it's more than that. It's still painful for me to recall those events and to accept again what I did and why I did it. Yet there is no escaping it and my need to relate it to you is crucial. I desperately want you to understand.

So, last week, I decided on an experiment. If I were to lie on my cot and close my eyes and concentrate, I might succeed in shutting out the existence of my cell and my thoughts of the coming trial and transport myself back to that night at Camp Jordan. If I could talk out my thoughts as they rose. . . . It was worth trying.

The next morning I asked my troubled lawyers for a tape recorder. I told them I wanted to record some answers to their questions that I had been unable to give them in direct conversation. They were elated, eager for any information that might help my case or, at the least, enlighten them. They secured the approval of the authorities and brought me a tape recorder two days ago. Since then, I have succeeded in taping those suppressed thoughts and yesterday I transcribed them in my journal and then erased the tape. At this moment I have no intention of giving the material to my lawyers. As I told you, I have no faith that it would help my case. That is for you to judge. My thoughts on the tape were somewhat confused and I have edited it only for clarity. This is the gist of it:

Thinking back to that night the images I see are not the three GI's I killed that afternoon but those Vietnamese prisoners huddled in that paddy. I can see that man lying on the ground, his trembling hands covering his head, his eyes stark with fear. And the rifle hovering at his head and his head bursting open. And those desperate women, clutching their screaming children, and being kicked and beaten and humiliated and laughed at. It sickens me in my gut. I can feel now the pain of guilt when I ran for the chopper and left them there knowing that the lieutenant and the troopers were going to shoot them. I keep thinking I could have done something to stop it. I didn't really try. I was too frightened for my own life to try and save theirs.

After we took off in the chopper, I don't think I had the intention of killing the lieutenant and the troopers. But I did search them out in that field and when I spotted them something inside my head clicked. I wanted to kill them.

149

I wanted to erase the guilt I had for failing those Vietnamese. I simply had to do it. I don't know how to explain how easy it was for me to shoot down those GI's in that field, but it was. It just happened.

I knew if I didn't stop them they would go on murdering and I would be guilty of letting them.

I remember now lying on my cot that evening and sweating because of what I had done. But it didn't last long. Concern for myself quickly enveloped me. I worried about what would happen when they found the dead GI's in the elephant grass, their bodies strafed with American bullets. Would there be an investigation? Would my pilot testify that I had fired my machine gun into the field when he hadn't seen anyone there? Throughout the night I had fantasies of a court martial at which I was called on to explain why I had fired on my own men. Would I tell them it was an accident? That I thought they were VC, as I had told my pilot? Or would I tell them the truth of all that had happened in that paddy? And would I tell them how Sergeant Stone had slit the throat of that innocent boy; how Corporal Doll had cut off the finger of the dead sniper; how Hammer had murdered the wounded boy and tried to murder me? Could they possibly understand? Could they confront our monstrous butchery?

I did not sleep that night but my worries came to nothing. There was no investigation into the deaths of the three GI's. There was no report of the murder of the Vietnamese detainees. There was only the report the next morning that the VC had been routed and their position in the tree line overrun. The dead were counted on both sides and the kill ratio was greatly in our favor and that was all that mattered. And the war went on and I went on with it.

○

One morning, a week after that mission, the camp hummed with talk of an incident that had happened the day before. It involved the colonel I had met in the rice paddy. Colonel Robert and his men were patrolling near a village when they had been fired on by a single sniper. No one had been hit, and because the village was listed as pacified the colonel had ordered his troops not to open fire on it. A methodical search for the sniper was conducted, and when a man was seen running from one of the hootches troopers cut him down and set fire to the hootch. The colonel came on the scene as a woman ran from the burning hootch and was instantly gunned down by two troopers. The colonel reacted furiously and on returning to camp he confined the men to quarters and reported the incident to the brigade commander. Colonel Wolfe, the brigade commander, belittled the incident, telling Colonel Robert that it was common practice for the troopers to destroy the hootch and kill the inhabitants for harboring an enemy. Colonel Robert was outraged at the failure of his superior to back him up. He insisted that the troopers be reprimanded for flagrantly disobeying orders. Colonel Wolfe refused and told him to forget the whole thing—that it was bad for morale to make an issue of it.

The general feeling in the camp supported Colonel Wolfe. What the hell was so terrible about killing a gook woman and burning a hootch? It was standard operating procedure. Colonel Robert damn well knew it. If that fucking sniper had come out of the hootch blasting away, he could have killed those GI's. What the hell would Colonel Robert have said about that? Hold your fire. Shit on that, man! Them fucking pacified villages are the worst. You don't know who the hell the enemy is or where he is. Next thing you know you got a pacified bullet in your head. They ought to light up every fucking gook hamlet in the country. That'd bring Charlie out in the open. Anyways, you know damn well them gooks'd kill our women and kids if they got the chance. They ain't got no bleeding Colonel Robert on their side. You know why? Because gooks ain't really human. They're nothin' but animals. Only difference is they can shoot so you got to kill them before they kill you. That's what it's all about, man—killing them. The body count is where it's at. You just got to figure their total population and keep on killing till the body count matches it. It ain't gonna be finished till then. Colonel Wolfe knows that. You can bet your ass when he sends the body count to division headquarters that gook woman'll be on it. Them troopers just did their job. It's that fucking Colonel Robert who's crazy. Hold your fire. For what? Till you see the whites of their slanty eyes? I don't want to go out on no patrol with Colonel Robert. If I was the brigade commander I'd put him in charge of keeping the body count. That'd keep him busy.

Amen.

The next day we heard that the two troopers had been given a verbal reprimand by Colonel Wolfe and returned to duty with their company. They were greeted with cheers.

Colonel Robert stubbornly persisted in his efforts to have the men punished, reporting the incident directly to the division commander. It got him an immediate transfer to a battalion in the north.

The outcome reinforced my view that it didn't pay to buck the system. If a colonel couldn't get a hearing of his charges then what chance did a door gunner have? Moreover, it was clear to me that the military command regarded killing "gooks" as normal procedure and not to was perverse.

Still, it wasn't that simple. The army functioned with a sympathetic understanding of the fears and tensions that burdened the combat soldier. Operating in an alien land, despised by a people and an enemy he didn't regard as human, his instinct for self-preservation often pushed him to acts of excessive brutality. His security depended on his buddies in the field and on his weapon. All else threatened him constantly and his obsessive fear for his life found its release in his trigger finger. The army understood that and accepted it as an essential hazard of its business. It was necessary to overlook the excesses in order to get the job done.

But, like Colonel Robert, I didn't fit into that scheme of things. I had no capacity for slaughter and I couldn't justify it. On the contrary, I felt a moral obligation to stop it. So, the army's solution in handling the protest of Colonel Robert had a profound effect on me: I became a shrewd enemy of the system. And thereafter, I was untroubled by a bad conscience and I acted dispassionately in the matter of killing.

8.

You may have read about the action I was involved in at the hamlet of Bong My. It was reported briefly in some of the newspapers two months ago—when I was already in prison—though it occurred eight months ago when I was more than halfway through my 365 days in Vietnam. The news took that long to surface because, according to one account, the Army managed to stifle it in "a conspiracy of silence." Other accounts said it was suppressed at the time because someone in high office decided that Americans at home were unable to endure another tragedy so soon after the horror and revulsion of the massacre at My Lai. Whatever the reason, the events at Bong My had a far lesser impact on the American conscience than the holocaust that struck My Lai. In the scale of things, that was understandable. The enormity of the My Lai massacre was almost beyond comprehension even for many of us fighting in Vietnam. Still, Americans should have been more disturbed, if less shocked, to learn what had happened at Bong My simply because it happened *after* My Lai. And if Americans desperately needed to regard the barbarity at My Lai as an awful aberration, Bong My made it clear that it was not.

Perhaps that is the real reason why the news of Bong My was suppressed for so long and received so little attention afterwards. Almost everyone wanted to believe that it didn't happen. But it did. I saw it. I was a part of it.

For me, the events of that day began at eight o'clock in the morning in the operations shack at Camp Jordan. My crew had been rounded up for an emergency mission at the bottom of the Delta. The briefing officer circled Bong My on the map and told us that D Company of the 4th Infantry Brigade was on its way there. Their orders were to make a sweep south through the area and clear it of VC. That part of the Delta had long been controlled by the VC and this was going to be the big push to drive them out. Bong My was the collecting point for the start of the sweep. It was selected because it sat at the apex of the VC stronghold and had been evacuated recently by the VC after they had forcibly recruited all the able-bodied men and stripped the hamlet clean of its rice stocks and supplies.

Our mission was to go into Bong My behind the transport choppers and stand by to give fire support to D Company when they called for it. Four other gunships were assigned to patrol the flanks of the VC position in support of two more companies. An attack of that size could only mean that the VC forces were expected to be strong and well entrenched, though the briefing officer was careful not to say so. It had become standard operating procedure not to estimate the total strength of the enemy at briefings. In recent months there had been several incidents of troops refusing to attack strongly held positions and the Army was hypersensitive about it. But nobody was fooled by the new procedure. We all knew that the size of our forces was determined by the size of the enemy force and the ratio greatly favored them.

By the time we took off from the base, the transports had a twenty-minute lead on us, but with our greater speed we came into Bong My less than ten minutes behind them. As we hovered over the landing zone, a grassy plain some two hundred meters from the hamlet, the empty transports were

155

revving up to depart and the troopers of D Company had already fanned out into three platoons and were moving across the field toward the cluster of thatched hootches glistening in the bright morning sun. There was no sign of inhabitants in the hamlet or the fields but the troopers approached cautiously. While we hovered, waiting for the transports to take off, I noticed something in the landscape that clearly indicated the VC had been there. Thirty meters from the hootches, the carcasses of two water buffaloes lay in a line across the narrow dirt road leading into the hamlet. Beside them, I could make out the small figure of a man or boy. My immediate thought was that the VC had slaughtered the animals at that spot to block the road. It was their practice to punish unfriendly villages by taking their crops and destroying their livestock. In this case, the dead buffaloes and the dead man completed the picture given by the briefing officer of a village terrorized by the VC. But where were the rest of the inhabitants? The village itself was unscarred. Were they hiding from us in their hootches? There was hardly a village in all of Vietnam that hadn't experienced terror and death from the VC or us and the sudden appearance of transports disgorging troops in battle gear at their doorstep would greatly alarm any villagers. They were the victims in the crossfire of a limitless guerrilla war. And, as I had seen, they couldn't even bury their dead in peace.

Constant fear for one's life was the overwhelming emotion everyone lived with: the VC knew it in the jungle and in their caves, the peasants knew it in their hootches and their fields, and we knew it in our gunships and on our patrols. Search-and-destroy missions were aptly named. It was the nature of the work. And the ones who feared it most were the peasants.

So that day at Bong My—as I was to learn—the villagers cowered in their hootches hoping that we would pass through quietly and leave them to go on with their lives. But it was not to be so.

Immediately after the transports lifted off and headed

back to the base, Sergeant Bright began the descent into the landing zone. At that moment, we heard gunfire popping above the roar of the motors. Off to the right, troopers in the center platoon, moving in a crouch on both sides of the road leading into the village, were firing sporadically, kicking up puffs of dust around the dead man and the buffaloes. They pumped thirty or more shots before the firing stopped. It seemed like a stupid thing to do, exploding bullets into a dead man and dead animals, but I was beyond trying to understand the trigger impulses of GI's. I was simply relieved that it wasn't enemy fire. But then we got trouble of our own.

We were coming in slow, hovering fifteen feet off the ground, when the rotors suddenly cut out and we dropped like a rock. The landing gear crumpled as we struck the ground. Both skids snapped like dry twigs and the ship shuddered as it tilted over on its belly. We were all badly shook up but unhurt. I got on the intercom. It was dead. It took us only seconds to realize the whole power system was out. Sergeant Bright had no explanation for it. Jonesy and I scrambled to the ground to inspect the damage to the undercarriage. It was flattened against the fuselage in a pancake of steel. Sergeant Bright and our copilot, Sergeant Leader, ran a check of the controls. Nothing worked, not that it mattered much. We couldn't have lifted off again because there was no way to set down safely without skids. Choppers aren't built to make a belly-landing more than once.

Our immediate concern was communication. With the radio dead we were out of contact with the base and the troopers. Sergeant Bright ordered me and Jonesy to report our condition to the commander of D Company. Another gunship had to be called in for fire support and we needed a Chinook chopper with a crane to lift us out of there. I didn't much like being a foot soldier again but there was no way out of it. Jonesy and I got our M-16's and ammo belts and took off after the troopers advancing on the village.

The dirt road was closest to our position and we made directly for it across the open field. I was anxious to catch the troopers before they reached the village and split up into smaller units. On the road we broke into a trot until we reached the dead buffaloes blocking our route. They were a mass of bleeding cuts where the bullets had ripped open their hides. The dead man turned out to be a small boy, his head shattered and his body shredded from the troopers' target practice. It was a sickening sight and I hurried past it and jogged on down the road with Jonesy beside me. Ahead of us, at the edge of the village, the troopers had spread out in pairs and were approaching the first row of hootches bordering the open field. One trooper was posted on the road about twenty-five meters from the hamlet. He turned in alarm, his rifle on us, as we came puffing up to him. He lowered his barrel.

"Where'd you guys come from?"

Jonesy identified us and told him what had happened to our chopper.

"Shit," the trooper said. "The lieutenant'll be sore as hell if we run into Charlie and we ain't got fire support."

"Yeah. That's why we got to find him in a hurry," Jonesy said. "Where's he at?"

The trooper pointed off to the left. "He's back there in the wood line with a squad to catch Charlie if he comes out this way after we go in."

"You expecting trouble here?" I asked. "We heard Charlie left this village and took all the men in it."

"Yeah. That's the poop but you saw them dead buffalo and that gook back there. This was a VC village and we got orders to light it up."

"Whose orders?"

"The lieutenant."

"What if there's women and kids still in there?"

"Anybody we find we're supposed to hold for interrogation."

"Listen, Glass," Jonesy said. "We better get going to the lieutenant. Is the radio operator with him?" Jonesy asked the trooper.

"Yeah. And there's another one in the village. This is a big sweep. We got two more platoons on the flanks."

"You going into the village?" I asked the trooper.

He shook his head. "I got orders to stay here on the road and pick up any civilians that come out."

"Maybe we better split up," I said to Jonesy. "I'll stay here and sweat out the radioman in the village. You report to the lieutenant. The quicker we make contact, the quicker we get our asses out of here. I'll meet you back at the ship in fifteen minutes."

"Right." Jonesy turned away and started across the field to the wood line eight hundred meters off to the left. I watched him until he disappeared in the high grass.

Suddenly, automatic gunfire erupted behind me. I hit the ground before looking back. The trooper was on his belly in the road, his rifle aimed at the village in the direction of the gunfire. It broke off and then began again in a steady tattoo but we couldn't see the action. In the hot sun of the morning, the hamlet still looked peaceful. Whatever the platoon had encountered was hidden from us. The gunfire kept us alert and tense.

More small-arms fire crackled off to the left and then on our right. It sounded like a full-scale firefight was going on in the village though we could see nothing of it. The trooper looked back at me in the road.

"Sounds like they found Charlie in there," he called out. I didn't answer him and he turned his attention back to the village.

We lay there waiting, watching. The gunfire increased. Forty meters ahead and on the left, three small figures appeared from behind one of the hootches and darted into the field. They were about fifteen meters into the field when a trooper came running from the village after them. At the edge of the field he stopped abruptly, dropped to one knee and quickly opened fire. All three figures hurtled through the air and flopped into the grass. Jumping up, the trooper raced to the spot and raked it with gunfire. I watched him

159

look down, remove his helmet and calmly wipe his forehead with his shirt sleeve. Then he put his helmet back on and walked slowly back to the village and disappeared behind a hootch. Seconds later, swirls of smoke arose from the hootch and the straw roof burst into flame. All this time, the gunfire continued steadily from every part of the village. It made me uneasy. There was something frightening and ominous about the situation. I sensed a violence in the air different from encountering the enemy in a firefight. There was no enemy to be seen and no sign of the villagers, except for the children cut down by the trooper. What the hell was the gunfire all about? If Charlie was in there how the hell could the trooper return so casually to the village showing no sign of caution?

I can still see him—all these months later—standing quietly over those three dead children and blasting away in the morning sun. I can see the bodies bouncing in the grass as the bullets tore into them. And I can see everything else that happened that morning as if it were only yesterday.

I can see the woman suddenly appearing in the roadway from the village, coming directly toward us in a half crouch, her arms huddling a child to her bosom, her head wagging from side to side as she frantically looked for a haven in that sunlit landscape, and then stopping motionless in the road as she caught sight of the trooper flattened in the dust, his rifle pointing at her and her head rearing back in that moment of panic just before the trooper opened fire at twenty meters and the bullets ripped open her arms and the child fell out on the road and she dropped onto it, still trying to shield it from harm. I can see her head lifting up from the dust of the road, her eyes staring at us, and the bullets kicking up dust in front of her and finally slashing into her head and ripping off the top of her skull.

I can see the trooper turning to me with a grin of satisfaction and reloading and turning back to wait.

I can see the big black trooper, a hulk of a man, coming out of the village, hobbling awkwardly on one good leg and

160

dragging the other, his whole body careening at every step. Despite his bad leg, he hurtled himself along the road in frantic flight and several times seemed about to topple headlong on the road only to regain his balance and plunge forward. I can see him approaching the dead woman crumpled over her child and hear him shouting "Jesus" and then stumbling around her and coming on again straight toward the aimed rifle of the trooper, who turned to look at me in bewilderment.

"That's Big Man. What the hell's going on?"

I couldn't talk to him. I kept my eyes riveted on the black trooper heaving toward us, sucking air into his mouth and panting, his face shining with sweat. Finally, he lurched up to the trooper and lowered his body to the ground and stretched out his injured leg. His broad, flat face was contorted in pain. I crawled over to them. The black trooper was muttering and shaking his head. The whole front of his foot was butchered and the blood oozing from it was covered with dirt.

I can see his huge chest heaving and hear him sobbing, still trying to catch his breath, and muttering over and over, "They gone crazy, man," and the tears streaming down from his black eyes and mingling with the sweat on his face and bubbling on his lips. And the trooper grasping him by the shoulders and asking him in a frightened, pleading voice, "What is it? What happened, Big Man?"

And Big Man shaking his head and blubbering, "They gone crazy. Wild crazy."

"Who? Charlie? He shoot you?"

And Big Man crying and shaking his head and then holding his hands over his ears as if he were stifling some sound inside his head.

And the trooper trying to shake him out of his shock and demanding to know how the hell he had been wounded: "You step on a mine, Big Man?"

And Big Man closing his eyes, squeezing off the tears, and swaying his head from side to side and sucking gulps of

161

air into his mouth and slowly calming down and opening his eyes and recognizing the trooper and shouting: "Mother-fuckers! Butchers!"

"He's crazy with pain," the trooper said to me. "We got to get him to the medics. He ain't himself."

I can see Big Man's face going hard—no more tears, no more shouting, only his black eyes still full of anger. I can hear that voice holding down the anger and spilling out the thoughts like a flowing river rising slowly and steadily until it reaches flood tide and plunges beyond its banks: "I'm myself, man. I'm all together. I ain't crazy with no pain. The foot don't bother me none. It's going to be all right. I did it myself. Self-inflicted, man. I blew off my foot steada blowing off my head. You understand? It was the only way I could get out of there and keep from going crazy." His eyes swept over us. "No mines, no Charlie, no nothin' but women and kids and old men with no teeth in their heads. That's all there is in that village. And they're getting beaten and killed and burned and raped by you white mother-fuckers of this here United States Army of Liberation. That's not my fucking war in there, man. I don't shoot babies. Nos-sir. They gonna have to kill me 'fore I do that. You under-stand me, man? We went into that village scared of Charlie only he ain't nowhere around. Nowhere. We didn't find nothing but hootches. 'Light 'em up,' the sarge says. 'Shoot them when they come running out.' And they do what he says. They went crazy."

I can see the swirls of smoke rising from the village behind Big Man as he sat in the road and talked, never turning his head. I can see the whole hamlet flaming into one huge bonfire and groups of women and children and some old men stumbling out into the fields and falling and rising again and running and the troopers right after them, raking the fields with gunfire, cutting them down—every one of them.

And Big Man talking away about the nightmare he'd been through and never turning his head toward the night-mare going on behind him: "A naked baby came crawling

162

out of this burning hootch bawling and screaming and the sarge come up to me and says, 'What the hell you looking at, Big Man? Shoot the bastard. This here's a VC village.' And I say, 'I ain't killing no naked baby, sarge. It ain't got no rifle, man.' 'Shit,' the sarge says and he pumps half a clip into the kid and just walks away. And when a young girl comes out of the next hootch, maybe ten years old, and her mother after her, and a trooper chops down the mother and then tears the pajamas off the girl and starts playing with her little bitty tits and pumping his muscle at her. The fucker had dropped his M-16 on the ground and she got away from him and ran for it. He just picked up his rifle and blew her head off and then he ran into the next hootch and started shooting it up. They was all doing the same thing—killing and raping and killing. That's when I put a bullet into my foot and got my ass out of there. It's worse'n hell, man, and ain't nothin' gonna get me back. You understand what I'm saying? You motherfucker, why'd you kill that woman and kid back there on the road? Huh? Why? You crazy, too? There's no VC there."

And I can see the fury exploding in his eyes and I can see his powerful arms lashing out at the trooper beside him on the ground and the huge fist cracking across the trooper's nose and sending him sprawling backwards into the road and the trooper scrambling to his feet and screaming "You black bastard!" and holding his rifle on Big Man, the barrel quivering in his hands.

And Big Man shouting: "You white motherfucker! What you gonna do?"

I can see the hate in the trooper's face and the blood running from his nose and hear his voice snarling, "You black gook!" and his rifle clicking a round into the chamber. "I got a mind to blow off your other foot. What the hell you want to hit me for?"

With the rifle on him, Big Man bristled. "What the hell you kill that woman for? She come at you with an AK? She threaten you?"

"I seen a trooper firing at gooks in the field. I figured

163

they're VC and then this woman come running at us so I fired. I'm supposed to kill gooks. That's what I'm here for."

"You supposed to hold civilians for interrogation. That was the fucking orders."

"Man, everybody's firing. I don't see them holding nobody for interrogation. Ain't you been telling me that?"

"They're crazy in there. Don't you understand nothin', man? They're killing everybody in that village and Charlie ain't in it."

"Shit. I ain't leading this platoon. We got orders to fire the village and clear it out."

"We ain't got no orders to slaughter women and kids."

"Since when you so fucking holy? You got more kills than any man in the platoon."

"VC, man. Charlie—the enemy. Not kids and women."

I can see the trooper shaking his head in disbelief and looking toward the village billowing smoke and flame and hearing the gunfire and wondering what the hell kind of madhouse he was in to be arguing with a crazy black trooper who'd shot off his own foot and had smashed him in the nose for no goddamn reason. He rubbed away the blood from his nose and looked at the red splotches on his fingers and the sight rekindled his anger.

"Get this crazy sonofabitch out of here or I'll kill him," the trooper said to me. "Take him back to the lieutenant. He'll bust his ass when he hears he shot off his own foot."

I can see Big Man's face breaking into that wide Uncle Tom grin, his mouthful of teeth showing a lot of gum. "Yeah, boy, take me to the lieutenant. Ah'm lookin' forward to tellin' him all about it. Matter of fact, Ah'm eager for that motherfuckin' court-martial. Eager, man." He kept grinning at the bloodied trooper. "Yeah, little man, Ah got the most kills in this motherfuckin' outfit and the most medals and Ah'm gonna tell them how I got them and how I got this busted foot and how you shot up a little old lady runnin' down the road with a pickaninny in her arms. Motherfucker!"

I can see Big Man's eyes flashing and his head going

164

back in a roar of wild laughter as he lay back flat in the dusty road and the sight of him howling and enraging the trooper, standing over him and cocking his rifle. "Shut up or I'll blow your fucking head off!"

And Big Man just laughing and closing his eyes. "Shoot, you motherfucker! Shoot! Ah'm waitin'."

And the trooper's barrel moving up the Big Man's body to his head and holding there. And I sat up straight in the road and held my rifle on the trooper and heard myself saying: "Let him be."

And I can see Big Man raising his head and looking up at the trooper, his eyes hard and cold and his voice spitting out the taunts: "Little man ladykiller! Little man babykiller!"

In that moment, I think he wanted to be shot.

I can see the trooper's rifle quivering at the Big Man's head and hear him shrieking, "You crazy, fucking black gook!" And I knew he was going to kill him.

I don't remember squeezing the trigger or hearing the shot but I can see the trooper's chest bursting open at that short range and his body falling forward and Big Man rolling over in the dust as the trooper went sprawling flat, face down, beside him.

○

I've had nightmares about it and they're always the same. The trooper screams, "You crazy, fucking black gook!" at me, not at Big Man, and then there's no sound at all and the trooper's chest erupts like the red petals of a poppy opening to reveal its black center in a kind of slow-motion movement and it grows larger and larger, looming toward me, blotting out everything else until it's smothering me and I wake up in an icy sweat. It's a strange nightmare because Big Man is never in it. For a long time it recurred and then it finally stopped until last night, in my cell, after I fell asleep thinking about the incident. Perhaps now that I've set it down in these pages, the nightmare will be gone for good.

165

O

After I killed the trooper I was too shaken up to hear what Big Man said to me. Mostly I remember him mumbling to himself and grinning at me in astonishment. I didn't understand why he was grinning. I thought he must be really out of his head. But he wasn't. He had all his wits about him. When he saw me looking in panic across the fields and back at the village, he knew where I was at.

"Nobody saw nothing but me, man. They all too busy doing their own killing."

"Maybe they saw us from the wood line," I said.

"You see them in the wood line?"

"No. The grass is too high."

"That's right, man. The grass is too high for them, too. Hey, man. Why'd you do it?"

"He was about to kill you. I had to stop him."

"You sure stopped him, man. But why? You never seen me before."

"I hated him when he cut down that woman and kid. He enjoyed it. But why'd you bait him like that? You were asking for it."

The grin dissolved on his face. "You hear that gunfire and the screaming? I guess it made me crazy. I wanted out. I got eleven months in Nam, man, but I never seen nothing like this before today. I can't take no more. I just want out from this misery."

"Well, you're out of it now with that foot. They'll ship you home."

"Nah. They gonna court-martial my black ass." He sat there in the road shaking his head, talking aloud, as if I weren't there. "I got a personal body count of thirty-two VC. You think that gonna matter to the man? All he gonna know is I shot off my foot. 'You disabled yourself, Big Man. You quit in the line of duty. Don't you understand that?' 'Yassuh, colonel, suh. I did wrong. I shoulda stayed there

166

and murdered them women and kids, suh. I did wrong, suh. Please, colonel, suh, don't be hard on me.'" Big Man looked intently up at me and his broad face ballooned into that wide grin. "Don't worry, man. We both gonna be all right. We gonna lick this motherfucking army."

"How do you figure that?"

"Give me a lift up." He extended his hand and I pulled him to his feet. He listed over on his good leg and loomed over me. He must have been six six or more. He looked back toward the burning village. It seemed like every hootch was afire. Billowing smoke obscured our view. There were no troopers to be seen. Those who had come out of the village to shoot down the fleeing villagers had returned to it. The gunfire was light, just a short burst now and then.

"They're moving south," Big Man said. "That's good." He looked at my shoulder patch. "You from that gunship?"

"Yeah."

"That's what I figured. How come you here?"

I told him what had happened to the chopper.

"I'm sure glad, man. You saved my crazy ass."

"Yeah, and I got mine in a sling."

"You just listen, man." He pulled two grenades from his belt. "I'm going to put these mothers under the little man here and pull the pins. He stepped on a mine, see? And it ripped the poor motherfucker apart. But I was lucky. It only blew off the front of my foot. That's it, man."

"You think they'll buy that?" I asked.

"When I go hobbling across that field screaming and bleeding with pain and they see my foot and I tell the man what happened he's gonna say, 'You got more lives than a black cat, Big Man.' He ain't gonna give a shit for this fucker 'long as he got an eyewitness report on him. And I'm the only eyewitness. By tomorrow my black ass'll be lying between clean sheets in the hospital ward in Saigon. Now you just get your ass back to your chopper while I take care of the little man here. Hustle, now."

"You'll need help to lift him."

"I don't need no help. Move off, man. You did your

167

bit. This is my show. The foot don't bother me none."

I put out my hand and he gripped it hard. "Thanks, Big Man."

"Yeah. We even up. See you after the revolution, Whitey —if you make it." And he laughed.

I left him laughing and started across the field on the right toward my gunship. I had gone about fifteen meters into the grass when the grenades exploded behind me. I looked back. The dead trooper was twisted in a heap a few feet from where I had killed him. Big Man was limping off in the high grass toward the wood line, moving fast on his bad foot. It was the last I ever saw of him. He must have made a convincing report to "the man" because I never heard anything of it. Much later I realized I had not told him my name. I was only "Whitey" to him. But he knew my face and if he's seen it in the newspapers or on TV since my notoriety, I like to think he said, "Goddamn, I know that white motherfucker! He's all right."

Where are you, Big Man?

○

As I told you, the slaughter at Bong My went unreported at the time, but two days after the action *Stars and Stripes* carried a short account of the operation in the Delta. I clipped it and still carry it with me. It reads:

> Three American infantry platoons of the Thirty-First Division in the Mekong Delta made a major sweep south of Bong My and despite stiff enemy resistance cleared the area, which has long been a VC stronghold.
>
> In the initial advance on Bong My, American troops encountered sporadic enemy fire but it quickly crumbled and the enemy forces fled south, taking up a strong defensive position in a wooded area bordering the rice fields.
>
> At Bong My, American casualties were light. One trooper was killed by a mine and another wounded when D Company, led by Lieutenant Butcher, over-

168

ran and liberated Bong My. In the course of the fire-fight, much of the hamlet was destroyed and its civilian inhabitants were rounded up for interrogation and subsequent relocation to safer areas.

At the wood line, gunships pounded the entrenched enemy positions for several hours before American troops moved in and destroyed the last pockets of resistance. At the time of this report, the known enemy dead toll is twenty-five but it is expected to rise when mopping-up operations have been completed. Two Americans were killed in the firefight and three wounded, bringing the total American casualties for the day's action to three dead and four wounded. Three gunships participated in the sweep and all returned safely.

The account failed to report that my gunship had a power failure and was lifted out of the area and returned to its base. I guess that wasn't considered news to anyone but my crew.

I don't know if the *Stars and Stripes* story was reported by the press at home. I do know when the full story of the Bong My massacre finally broke two months ago because of the persistent digging of a Midwest reporter, the Army announced it was ordering a full investigation of the events. Since then, though I read the newspapers hungrily every day in my prison cell, I have seen nothing more about it. The Army's investigation seems to be a well-kept secret and I suspect its findings will be equally secret. Why not? Nobody seems to care. If My Lai was an extraordinary revelation, it is not something this country would want to reveal again. Is it?

When I think back to how alarmed I was for my own safety because of what I had done that day, I realize I was foolish. If a whole village could be burned to the ground and all its inhabitants murdered without causing a ripple of concern, then I had nothing to fear. Big Man had understood that. I can still see him laughing in the road outside that burning slaughterhouse.

169

9.

○

I was fortunate that Big Man was the only witness to any of the killings I had committed. But the day I killed the general there was another witness and he was hostile. The circumstances were bizarre but in Vietnam the bizarre is routine.

○

Every war has a Patton. In Vietnam, it was red-haired Brigadier General George Rusty Gunn, the area division commander. I did not know him firsthand. Even in Vietnam, the chasm between a general and a private is wide. But everyone knew him by reputation. He ran a tough outfit, keeping a tight leash on his chain of command and weeding out any mavericks who didn't mesh with his gung-ho style. His brisk transfer of Colonel Robert was typical. ("The old man doesn't take any shit. He only dishes it out." The remark summed up the man.) Rusty Gunn had earned his star in the field doing everything he asked of his men. He was fond of saying, "You don't push your men into combat. You lead them." But after he got his star, he did more pushing and less leading.

170

His division had the highest kill record for the first quarter of '69 and it was a matter of record in every outfit in the country. Officers envied him but the GI's hated him. His methods were ruthless. He had abandoned the standard tactics of making contact with the enemy and then pulling back while the ground artillery and the gunships pummeled the enemy positions. His command was ordered to engage the enemy, no matter the odds, and demonstrate that GI's could destroy the enemy in close combat without artillery and air power. Only this way, the general reasoned, could the enemy be kept from dispersing and regrouping. Only this way would the GI become combat-hardened and know that he could beat Charlie on his own ground. The practice worked but at great cost in American lives. When companies were wiped out, fresh companies were committed. Firefights raged at close quarters on a tactical scale unknown in Vietnam. Whole platoons were slaughtered on both sides. Evacuation of the wounded was eliminated during the push. The wounded endured or died. That's the way it was. And it was a holocaust. American casualties were high but enemy casualties were higher. The kill ratio was General Gunn's game. He sat in his headquarters and pushed and totaled and totaled and pushed. And as long as his outfit moved forward, clearing the terrain of the enemy, nobody shortened his leash. It was the first time in the history of the war that an American commander had taken ground consistently and held it. Isn't that the way we did it in World War II? Isn't that the way wars are won? Isn't that the only way? To hell with the cost! If the enemy stands fast, kill them! If they retreat, chase them and kill them! Don't let them disperse and regroup. Push! Push! Push!

By the time I met General Gunn there wasn't a GI in his division who wouldn't have seized the opportunity to put a live grenade under the general's pillow. But the opportunity to kill a general is rare. It came to me quite unexpectedly. I could not have killed General Gunn without provocation. Having read this far in my journal, you must believe that. Though I had heard the common gossip of the general's

171

brutality, I had no personal knowledge of it. So, when my crew was ordered to fly the general on an aerial survey of the combat areas in the Delta, I considered the assignment routine and safe. It turned out to be neither.

○

Our assignment began early one morning in April—to be exact, April 20, 1969—nine months to the day of my arrival in Vietnam. I remember now telling my crew I had only three months left of my tour. They envied me because they had six months more to go. It surprised me to realize I was the veteran, because they had been flying together when I had joined them as a replacement. But I had put in my brutal time as a trooper when they were still flying practice missions in the States. And I remember, too, that long-ago morning of my first patrol with Blondy and Corporal Doll. Blondy had 333 days at the time and Doll had 200 days and three rivers behind him. And here I was with 275 days, still behind my friend Blondy but ahead of Corporal Doll, who had crossed his last river.

At nineteen I was the "old man" of my chopper crew, and now I felt the burden of time still ahead and it gave me a pang of fear. I imagined someone back home at the orphanage asking, "I wonder what ever happened to David Glass?" and someone answering, "Didn't you know? He died in Vietnam." I wanted desperately to escape that poor epitaph, and the weight of those remaining ninety days oppressed me that morning on the flight to our rendezvous with General Gunn at his division headquarters in the Delta.

General Gunn and his adjutant, Colonel Clay, were at the landing strip when we set down promptly at eight-thirty. The introductions were brisk and formal and we were back in the air in minutes and on our way to survey the combat areas. From my position behind my machine gun I observed the back of the general, seated on the deck at the open door. Colonel Clay was seated opposite him, obediently agreeing with everything he said. From time to time, General Gunn examined the map spread out on his lap and came on the intercom to Sergeant Bright with the coordinates of an area he wanted to investigate. At each checkpoint we circled low while the general scrutinized the terrain through his binoculars. When there was no evidence of combat activity we proceeded to the next checkpoint, crisscrossing the Delta, serene and lush below us. There was nothing in all that quiet landscape to indicate the presence of war. If men were killing men on that checkerboard of green rice paddies divided by brown strings of water, it was not apparent to the eye. After a while, it began to seem that the general's mission was to study not the activity of the war but the absence of it. I didn't know how he felt about the tranquillity in that countryside but I was most content. I had no reason to fire my machine gun. It was a most pleasant way to record my two hundred and seventy-sixth day in Vietnam—a day without violence, a day without death. But it was not to be so. It was to be the day that General George Rusty Gunn died in Vietnam.

We had logged three hours in the air when Sergeant Bright informed the general that we would soon have to return to the base to refuel. The news disgruntled the general. For the last hour he had been complaining about not seeing any signs of combat on the ground. Several times we had swooped in low over the areas he had marked on his map indicating battle zones only to see small knots of our troops bivouacked in positions where the enemy was supposed to be. If Charlie was anywhere about, he remained hidden. Once we came on a patrol plodding wearily through the high grass surrounding a ravine and the general raised them on the radio and requested a report of their mission. He was told that they were there to flush out the VC reported to be in the ravine but they had gone through it and found no sign of Charlie except for a series of abandoned tunnels. The general ordered them to request an air strike to blast the tunnels "and seal up any gook bastards hiding in there."

It was right after that when he gave Sergeant Bright the

course to take back to the base. "We're going to refuel and find the goddamn war if it takes all day. Sergeant, stay down at treetop level. I want to study the terrain closely on the way home."

Sergeant Bright responded, taking the chopper down on the deck across the open paddies and climbing only to clear the wooded areas.

"That's the boy," the general barked over the intercom. "Keep it down."

I watched the general as he leaned forward eagerly at the open door, his head swaying as he scanned the ground through his binoculars. He was determined to find something and he did. We had crossed a rice paddy and started to climb to clear the village dead ahead when the general's voice crackled on the intercom: "Sergeant."

"Sir?"

"Circle back wide to the left and come across the paddy again. Same course, same height."

"Something wrong, sir?"

"Nothing wrong, sergeant. Just want another close look."

"The fuel gauge is pretty low, sir."

"How much flying time, sergeant?"

"Fifteen minutes, sir. But I don't like to cut it too tight."

"Circle back, sergeant."

"Yes sir."

Sergeant Bright wheeled the chopper in a wide arc to the left. We had passed over the hamlet.

"Take it slower, sergeant. When you reach the far end of the paddy I want you to hover until I give you the go-ahead. Then I want you to take it across that rice field smooth and slow. You got that?"

"Yes sir. But if I know what you're looking for, sir, it would help."

"I'll tell you when I'm ready, sergeant."

"Yes sir."

As we flew wide of the paddy I kept my eyes on the general. He was chattering with Colonel Clay but I couldn't hear what they said above the whir of the rotors. Whatever

174

the general said, though, the colonel nodded in agreement.

Finally, the general put aside his binoculars and pulled his forty-five from his holster and pointed it toward the ground and steadied his aiming arm with his left hand. I didn't understand what he was doing but it fascinated me. Then he shook his head, replaced the pistol in his holster, and came on the intercom: "Sergeant, is there an M-16 on board?"

"Yes sir. The gunners carry them at all times."

"Good. I want one."

"You hear that, Glass?"

"Yes, sarge."

"Leave your station and give the general your M-16."

"Right."

I locked my machine gun, removed my earphones, picked up my M-16 and took it to the deck and handed it to the general. He grasped it and set it on automatic. It had a full clip. I started to return to my station but the general indicated for me to sit on the bench beside him. "Stay right here, son," he shouted above the roar of the blades. "We don't need a gunner for this."

I sat down beside him, puzzled at what the hell he was about, and looked across at Colonel Clay, who gave me a half-nod and a half-smile that told me nothing.

At the far end of the paddy, Sergeant Bright circled down to around fifty feet and hovered there.

"That's good, sergeant," the general said. "Now when I say go, I want you to take it straight across the paddy toward the left edge of the village. Hold it at your slowest possible airspeed. Halfway across, you will see three VC in the paddy off to the right. Keep them well on the right so I can get a clear bead on them. You got that, sergeant?"

Without my earphones I couldn't hear the sergeant's reply but I could see that it irritated the general. Scowling, he said testily, "I know VC when I see them, sergeant. There are three gooks in black pajamas down there. I don't give a damn if they're planting rice. They don't fool me. Now you put this chopper on course and take it slow."

175

From my position, I could see Sergeant Bright shaking his head. Then he gunned the engine and we spurted forward across the paddy. At the same moment, General Gunn raised my M-16 and held it steady, fixed on the open field below.

At my gun station, I had seen the peasants in the field on the first pass over. As far as I could tell, they were villagers planting rice shoots. They weren't armed and they hadn't bothered to look up as we passed over them. That was characteristic of the peasants. They had learned long ago to accept the war about them. VC would have hid themselves at the first sight of a chopper. The general had to know that. He had a lot more time in Vietnam than I did. But he was out for blood. The day had been too peaceful for a war lover and he wasn't about to let it pass quietly. I saw the whole scheme in the smug grin on Colonel Clay's face. At that moment I wanted desperately to frustrate them. But how? If I were flying the chopper I could wobble the ship to upset the general's aim but I knew that Sergeant Bright would obey his orders. He had learned to live with the brutalities of the war better than I had. All I could do was sit there beside General Gunn and watch him track the field through the scope of my rifle.

"That's it. Perfect," the general said gleefully to himself.

I raised myself up on the seat to peer over his shoulder. From my angle I saw the rifle barrel shift to the right and then I spotted the peasants ahead of us, bent over the rice shoots, their straw hats nodding in the sunlight. We were starting to pass them, no more than sixty meters away and fifty feet below. They never paused in their work to look up. Leaning far forward in the open door, the general opened fire. He caught them in the first long burst and all three black figures dropped to the ground. He continued to fire off the full clip. Colonel Clay, his gaze fixed intently on the line of fire, clapped his hands. "You got them, general."

General Gunn peered back at the scene and then turned

176

to his adjutant, his face gleaming with pleasure. "You know something, Clay. Killing gooks gives me a hard-on."

The colonel laughed. "I know just what you mean, general," he said and he closed his hands over his crotch.

Grinning, the general looked over his shoulder at me and winked. He was still leaning forward in the open door. I regarded him impassively and then I pressed my side up against him and thrust my weight behind my right shoulder and pushed hard. General Gunn toppled through the open door and disappeared without making a sound.

Even now I can see the look of stark amazement on the face of Colonel Clay. His mouth fell open in shock. It lasted a moment. I cracked my fist full into his nose, and as his head rolled back from the blow I bent forward and grasped his feet at the ankles and upended him through the opening, seconds behind his general.

It was done.

I sat perfectly still on the deck and gazed blankly at the square of space where the general and his adjutant had disappeared. That's when the shock hit me. My hands began to shake and I clasped them tightly. Finally, I looked around the ship. Sergeant Bright and the copilot were busy at the controls, pulling the ship up sharply as we headed over the village. Behind me, on my left, Jonesy sat hunched over his machine gun. None of them seemed aware of what had happened. I got to my feet. The tension in my chest felt like a vise. I went back to my position behind my gun and put on my earphones.

Sergeant Bright's voice was irritable: "General Gunn. Can you hear me? Come in."

When there was no answer, Bright turned to look back at the empty deck. I didn't wait for his next question.

"The general's not on board," I said.

"Where the hell is he? Where's the colonel?"

"They just fell overboard."

"What the hell are you talking about? How the hell could they fall overboard?"

177

We had crossed over the village and were heading north toward the base. The copilot was handling the controls. Sergeant Bright peered back at me from the cockpit.

"What the fuck happened back there, Glass?"

"I didn't see the whole thing."

"What the hell did you see?"

My voice sounded nervous but I figured that was all right. "I was watching the peasants in the paddy when the general fired at them. Next thing I know, the general was leaning way the hell out of the door to see if he got them. He must have slipped or something. I heard him yell and then he was falling out of the ship. The colonel made a grab for him and lost his balance and fell out, too."

"Jesus Christ! Holy Mother of God!"

There was a heavy silence on the intercom. Despite the wind blowing through the ship, I broke out in a nervous sweat. Finally, the copilot's voice came on: "I didn't hear nothing but them rotors. What the hell are we gonna do, sarge? Do we go back and look for them?"

"I don't know. I can't believe it. Let me think. Holy shit!"

After a few seconds Sergeant Bright said, "I'll take over the controls. We'll return to the base. We don't have enough fuel to go back and set down and get off again. And there might be VC down there. Mark the coordinates of the paddy and record the time. We're only about ten minutes from the division base. We'll just about make it."

We flew on in silence for several minutes. The tension eased in my chest and the cool wind dried the sweat on my face.

"Jonesy, you there?"

"Here, sarge."

"You heard the poop?"

"Every word."

"What'd you see?"

"Nothing, sarge. I couldn't see nothing from my side."

"You see them peasants in the field?"

"No, sarge."

"Glass."

178

"Yeah, sarge."

"Did the general hit those gooks in the paddy?"

"I think so. I saw them drop."

"They look like VC to you?"

"They looked like villagers planting rice to me."

"That's what I told the fuck but he wouldn't listen. Look what it got him."

"Yeah."

"Shit. We're going to be in big trouble when head-quarters hears we lost old Rusty Gunn and his adjutant. They'll have our ass."

"It ain't your fault, sarge," Jonesy said. "You told him we were low on fuel. You didn't want to make that pass over the paddy. I heard you tell him they was just farmers. I heard you."

"Me, too," I lied.

"I heard it, too," the copilot said.

"Good. Just remember everything when they start questioning us. Especially you, Glass. They're going to pump you because you saw the whole thing."

"I'll tell them just what happened."

"Don't let them rattle you. Stay cool."

"I'm cool, sarge."

"You said you heard the general yell?"

"Yeah."

"I didn't hear nothing over the rotors except the gunfire."

"Yeah," I said.

"How come you didn't come on the intercom when you saw them fall out?"

"It all happened so fast, sarge. And then you were raising the general right when it happened."

"You blew my mind, Glass. I still can't believe it."

"Me neither."

"The stupid sonofabitch. What a dumb way to die."

I thought about that for a moment and it gave me a jolt. Until that second, I hadn't considered that the general or the adjutant might still be alive in that paddy field. Could they have survived that drop? We were down pretty low.

I couldn't resist raising the possibility. "Maybe he's still alive, sarge. It wasn't too big a drop and those rice paddies aren't hard ground."

"No chance, Glass. I thought about that. We were at eighty feet coming across that paddy."

"I thought we were lower."

"No sir. If those gooks turned out to be VC with AK's, I wasn't about to give them a potshot at our gearbox. The general was playing games but not me. I even gunned it a bit. Didn't you notice? I wasn't about to put my ass on the line for that bastard. As it is, he fucked us good."

"Then you figure he had it?"

"You know the speed of a falling body? From eighty feet the general hit that paddy at more than sixty miles an hour. He couldn't possibly have survived the impact. Anyway, we'll find out soon enough. When headquarters gets the news they'll probably send out a whole fucking squadron to pick them up. Shit! It ain't every day you lose a general in this fucking war and a gung-ho general at that. He had the best kill record in Nam. Man, they're gonna eat us alive for this fuckup."

"We didn't fuck up, sarge," Jonesy said. "We just followed orders. Who the hell could have figured this would happen? It's a freak accident."

"That's what worries me. Who's gonna believe it was a freak accident? Goddamn that trigger-happy bastard."

"Don't beat yourself up," the copilot said. "We didn't do nothing but follow orders."

"Yeah, that's right," Sergeant Bright said with new confidence. "Fuck them all! Just tell it the way it is and stick to it. You all understand that?"

"Don't worry about us, sarge," Jonesy said.

"Man, what a surprise they're gonna get," Sergeant Bright said.

"Maybe we should radio headquarters and report what happened," the copilot said. "What do you think, sarge?"

"That'd be the dumbest thing we could do," Bright exploded. "We don't say nothing over the radio. We don't

180

know who the hell might pick us up and spread the goddamn story. We can't let this out to nobody but *his* staff
officers or they'll grind us into shit. Don't you know that
Rusty Gunn's the Pentagon's golden boy? Jesus Christ!"

"I wasn't thinking about that, sarge," the copilot said.

"Well, stop thinking and keep your eyes on that goddamn gas gauge. It's almost empty. Shit! That's all we need
is a forced landing in the boondocks and it'll be a complete
one-hundred-percent fuckup."

After that we flew on in silence and the fuel lasted us
into the base where we had picked up the general that
morning. We'd only been out four hours but it seemed like
the longest mission of my life when we finally climbed out
of the chopper and headed for the command tent. Only
Jonesy stayed behind with the ship to be certain that no
one serviced it. Sergeant Bright didn't want the ship re-
fueled until the brass had verified the empty gas gauge. By
the time we reached headquarters, I was sweating again
from the tension mounting in me. Under the circumstances,
I welcomed the intense heat of the afternoon sun because
the others were sweating as well.

○

As Sergeant Bright had anticipated, the brass hassled us
but the interrogation was brief. Initially, there was the
shock of Gunn's staff at our news; it was followed by their
skepticism of Sergeant Bright's explanation and my eyewitness account; then threats of an official investigation; and
finally they tried to destroy our testimony. It all added up
to zero. There were four of us with a corroborating account
and they had no evidence to disprove it—unless they found
the general or his adjutant still alive. When Sergeant Bright
raised that possibility, it brought their interrogation to an
abrupt end. Everyone had assumed they were dead. Suddenly, the recovery of the general and Colonel Clay—alive
or dead—became the immediate priority and the command
tent exploded in a flurry of activity. Three gunships, fully
armed, each with a complement of six troopers, were quickly

activated. Sergeant Bright was ordered to lead the gunships to the scene. Three staff officers—two colonels and a major—rode with us. Within half an hour of our arrival we were back in the air, including the time it took to refuel our ship after Sergeant Bright made certain the staff officers had verified our empty fuel gauge.

The flight to the rice paddy took twelve long, excruciating minutes. We circled down to two hundred feet and quickly spotted the bodies of the three peasants. Several hundred meters beyond them toward the village, another body was seen. Sergeant Bright picked out a field of low grass fifty meters farther on for a landing zone and we went in. The three gunships set down in a semicircle around us. We hurried to the spot with the armed troopers right behind us. The body of Colonel Clay lay spread-eagled, face down. One of the staff officers turned him over. His skull was split open from the top of his forehead to his chin. At the sight of his smashed face, I had the thought that they would have to ship him home in a sealed coffin.

The troopers fanned out across the paddy to search for the general. When they found him, a hundred and fifty meters from the body of his adjutant, a trooper called out that he was dead. We scurried over to them. General Gunn lay on his back. His face, unmarked, was contorted in rage. I noticed that his hands were clenched. Were they a last defiant gesture against me, I wondered, or against the death that had awaited the end of his fall? It did not matter now. I only knew that he would receive a nation's tribute and a hero's burial.

The same would not be true of the three black-clad peasants lying dead in their rice field, their backs pockmarked with the bullets fired by General Gunn. When the troopers kicked them over on their backs and removed their conical straw hats, we saw the worn, wrinkled faces of three old women.

○

On our return to division headquarters with the bodies of General Gunn and his adjutant, we were immediately cloistered again with the brass. They were no longer interested in interrogating us. The death scene in the paddy had changed the total focus of their concern. One of the colonels did all the talking. He said that if the press learned that General Gunn "had mistakenly killed" three women rice farmers there would be "hell to pay through the whole chain of command." It would take in everybody from the commanding general to the gunship crew. Was that clear?

It was clear.

There was to be no talk of General Gunn's aerial survey that morning by anyone. Was that understood?

It was understood.

The official account of General Gunn's death would be made by the Commanding General's Office in Saigon. The official report was all we would know about it. Was that clear?

It was clear.

As far as the record was concerned we had not flown that mission that morning. It had been scrubbed several hours after our arrival at division headquarters. Our commanding officer would be briefed by the time we returned to our base.

At that point, the colonel checked his watch. "I'll need an hour to lock this up and then you can take off. That'll make it fifteen hundred hours. You can get some chow while you wait. Any questions?"

My crew members shook their heads but I had a question: "What about my M-16, sir?" It had been found a few feet from the general's body by one of the troopers and the colonel had taken it and carried it back with him. He had been careful to hold it by the end of the barrel. We had all noticed that but it didn't worry me. I knew when they checked it out they'd find the general's fingerprints all over the stock, the barrel and the trigger.

The colonel regarded me impassively. "We'll keep it. You'll be issued a new weapon. I'll take care of that."

"Yes sir."

The colonel scowled at all of us. "One more thing, gentlemen. If any of you says one goddamn word about what happened today to anyone, you'll wish you were dead. Is that clear?"

It was clear.

"All right, gentlemen. The incident is closed."

And it was.

By the time we returned to our base, operations had received the word from division headquarters. Sergeant Bright turned in our flight log personally to the commanding officer with no questions asked. The next morning I was issued a new rifle with no questions asked. And two days after the event *Stars and Stripes* carried a headlined account of how the general had died in Vietnam. On a routine flight of the battle zones, his chopper had been shot down by enemy ground fire in a remote area of the Delta. There were no survivors but all the bodies had been recovered. The names of the crew members were being withheld until their families were notified. To my surprise, the story carried a picture of the wreckage of a chopper in a rice paddy. Of course, downed choppers were easy enough to fake but I wondered if the army had to create a fake telegram to send out to the imaginary families of an imaginary crew. Why not? Anything was possible in this absurd war—anything.

General Gunn's body was being flown to the States for burial in Arlington Cemetery with full military honors befitting a hero of the Republic. There was a summary story of the general's career with the usual quotations of the famous extolling the dedication of America's "most brilliant combat officer in Vietnam." A hawk Senator called him "God's general in the fight for freedom," and the President said, "He died as he had lived—in the service of his country."

Amen.

I put down the paper and breathed the hot, humid air of Vietnam more easily and smoked some grass. I was off the hook.

Amen.

God's general died in the service of his country with a hard-on.

Amen.

O

Which brings me to the close of my Vietnam year in the matter of killing.

O

Our chopper crew was transferred to a medical evacuation unit and I spent the remaining eighty-seven days of my year ferrying the wounded and the dead from the battle zone to the field hospital. It was gut-sick work and I survived the whole time on grass. Without it I would have gone mad listening to the screams of the maimed, the blind, the paralyzed. I still hear the cries of those butchered boys pleading to be shot. Only the dead were quiet.

Amen.

On the twenty-first of July, 1969—a year and a day after my arrival—I left Vietnam for the States.

Amen.

10 ○

On my return to the States I was given a sixty-day furlough (the reward of Vietnam veterans) before taking up my new assignment as a gunnery instructor at a base in Arizona. Soldiers go home on leave but the only home I had known was the Denver orphanage and it did not beckon to me. I had no friends there or anywhere else. I thought of trying to find Blondy but where was Cuntsville, the U.S. of A.? And there was Big Man. He must be home by now. I wanted to tell him how General Gunn had died in Vietnam. He'd appreciate that. But where was he?

I spent the first days of my furlough hanging around the army base at San Diego. I didn't know what else to do with my time. Though I hated it, the army was the only home I had now. Finally, out of boredom, I went back to the orphanage in Denver. It was a painful experience. The only staff people I wanted to see—the black cook, a woman who loved children, and an athletic instructor who had wanted me to become a professional baseball player—were gone. And only the director remembered me. He was a kind man and he treated me like a returning hero. He was proud of my service in the war and at a special assembly of the orphan boys he introduced me as a fine, patriotic American who had fought to preserve the ideals of our country. His effusive praise upset me and later, when the boys questioned me for exciting stories of my experiences, I told them I couldn't talk about it. The disappointment in their eager faces, so hungry for heroics, alarmed me.

The orphanage was an alien world to me and after two days I fled.

I went to the airport and checked the board of departing flights. I had to go somewhere for the remaining fifty-five days of my furlough. But where? There were night flights to Chicago and New York. Both appealed to me. Both were big cities in which I could get lost—simply exist in limbo until the army reclaimed me. I finally decided on the New York flight. I chose New York because it had been the home of my parents—a place where I had lived. Perhaps I hoped that I would find something of my past that would comfort me. But I found nothing. New York was totally strange to me and I did not have the security and protection of the army there. For the first time in my life, I was completely on my own and it frightened me.

I took a room at the YMCA. I slept away the daylight hours—it was a great luxury not to get out of bed in the morning after a year of army reveilles—and roamed the city by night. I spent the early evening hours in dark movie houses and the late hours in dark bars. I met the lonely night people: the alcoholics, the pimps, the whores and the men who didn't want to go home and the women who didn't want to go home alone. My uniform attracted them, and when they learned I had been in Vietnam they wanted to know all about it. I smoked grass and told them about fire-fights (no, it wasn't fighting fires) and slicing off fingers and ears and toes. They didn't believe me but they were fascinated and urged me on. I purged myself of all the atrocities I had seen. They were exhilarated. Have another drink, kid, on me. Tell me more, kid. You're too much. And I sucked on the joint and told them I had personally fought with General Gunn—and don't tell anyone about this, but General Gunn always had a hard-on before a battle. They loved that. It made them absolutely gleeful. General Gunn was a fucking hero—hah hah! You don't fuck the enemy without a hard-on. Right, kid?

○

Two weeks after my arrival in New York, the absurd telegram arrived in a special-delivery letter from the director of the orphanage. I had written him earlier explaining my sudden departure as a pilgrimage to find my childhood. He had replied promptly and said he hoped my search would be fruitful but that whatever happened there would always be a place for me at the orphanage when I needed it. I was touched by his decency and one night, after smoking grass in my room at the Y, I began a letter of confession to him, recounting the details of my Vietnam year. I never finished it. I could not shatter his dream of the war hero and he could not console me. He was not my father. My father was dead. After a long night of hallucinations, I awoke and destroyed the letter. I thought I was severing myself from my past. I was alone in the world and I had to accept it. There was no one to understand me; no one to give me absolution. That morning, for the first time since my childhood, I cried for myself, for my aloneness, and afterward I felt refreshed, as if I had vomited out the past, as if it were gone forever.

From this day forward . . .

My parents are dead; I will not think about them; I am an orphan man.

And I will not think about the year in Vietnam; it is dead and gone.

And I will not see that boy lying on the riverbank with his throat slashed.

Nor Hammer shooting that boy in the field.

Nor . . .

But the telegram destroyed my resolve to throw off the past. Forwarded to me, unopened, from the orphanage in a letter from the director expressing the hope that it bore good news, it instantly, vividly, recreated the experiences of my Vietnam year.

The telegram, as you know, was from the Secretary of Defense informing me that I had been awarded the Medal of Honor for extraordinary valor in combat. It seems that I had destroyed an enemy machine-gun emplacement and killed four of the enemy to save the lives of an American patrol, etc. etc.

As I reported at the outset of this journal, my response to this news was to laugh aloud. It was a monumental screw-up. Me, awarded the Medal of Honor; invited with my family to the White House to be decorated personally by the President. With my family!

The laugh died in my throat. I lit a joint to steady myself and stared at the telegram for a long time, rereading every word:

PRIVATE DAVID GLASS, THE DENVER HOME FOR ORPHAN BOYS, DENVER COLORADO. . . .

A long pull on the joint and I was at the White House gate with my family—all the orphan boys of the Denver Home. The director proudly had them lined up in their Sunday best in neat rows of twos. The White House guard, flustered, studied the telegram. He had to check it with his superiors. Yes, it was okay. I could go in with my family but first everyone had to be searched for weapons. The boys' penknives and cowboy guns were confiscated.

AS SECRETARY OF DEFENSE IT IS MY PLEASURE TO INFORM YOU THAT YOU HAVE BEEN AWARDED THE MEDAL OF HONOR FOR. . . .

For killing Private Hammer; for killing Lieutenant "Flyboy" and the Corporals Wade and Hawley; for killing General Hard-on and Colonel Yessir; for listening to the cries of the wounded and the silence of the dead; for enduring the shattered skulls, the slit throats, the severed fingers, ears, toes . . .

HEROISM IN BATTLE ABOVE AND BEYOND THE CALL OF DUTY IN DEFENDING THE LIVES OF YOUR PATROL BY DE-STROYING AN ENEMY MACHINE-GUN EMPLACEMENT AND KILLING FOUR OF THE ENEMY WITHOUT REGARD FOR YOUR

189

SAFETY. IN RECOGNITION OF YOUR VALOR, THE PRESIDENT REQUESTS YOUR PRESENCE WITH YOUR FAMILY AT THE WHITE HOUSE ON AUGUST 28 AT TEN A.M. TO ACCEPT YOUR AWARD.

Dear Mr. Secretary of Offense: I am in receipt of your telegram informing me that I have been awarded the Medal of Honor, and while I am overwhelmed by such recognition of my modest achievements in Vietnam I am also amused and worried: amused because your computers really fucked up in the selection of a hero; worried because I am a hero but not by your rules of conduct becoming a soldier. On the other hand, perhaps the computer in charge of selecting heroes is wiser than we are and has correctly picked me for this honor. So, I accept the honor and with my large family I will present myself at the White House on the day and hour designated. Yours, in the crusade to legalize marijuana, Private David Glass.

○

The teletypist at the Western Union office eyed me suspiciously as he sniffed the sweet smell of the joint before glancing at the handwritten blank I had handed him. He scowled. "You're supposed to print your message, not write it out." He looked at me through old-fashioned wire glasses. He was elderly and hostile.

"I'm sorry," I said. "If you can't read my handwriting, I'll do it over."

He studied the message again and read aloud: "Secretary of Offense." He looked up at me. "You mean Secretary of Defense, don't you?"

"No. You read it right." I grinned. He wasn't amused. "Read the rest of it," I said.

He proceeded to read the message to himself, his lips forming each word as he tracked them with his finger. Halfway through he stopped and scowled again. "You can't use cuss words in a telegram."

"What cuss words?"

"Four-letter words."

190

"Did I use a four-letter word?"

"Don't wise-ass me, son. I don't want no trouble."

"I'm not making any trouble. I just want to send my telegram."

He thumped at the message with his finger. "You can't say 'fucked up.' It's against the law."

"That's two words. Neither of them has four letters."

A sudden, frightened look came into his eyes as they moved from my face down my uniform. I realized he was looking to see if I was armed.

"I'm not looking for trouble. I just want to send this telegram to my commanding officer in the Pentagon. How about 'screwed up' instead of 'fucked up'?" I pulled a last puff from the joint and killed it on the floor. The old man became blurry. I was flying badly—the boy on the riverbank was looking at me with that terrible fear in his eyes. I closed my heavy lids. From far off, I heard the voice of the teletypist echoing off the walls. His tone was gentle.

"You're stoned, son. Why don't you go back to your room at the Y and sleep it off? I'll be here tomorrow."

I blinked at him. "You don't believe me. Here, I'll show you." I fumbled in the breast pocket of my tunic and pulled out the crumpled telegram from the Pentagon and pressed it flat on the counter.

As he read it, I swayed to other terrible images. I wasn't stoned enough. The poor, simple-minded old fart extended the telegram to me. "That's a great honor, son. I don't rightly know what's troubling you but you don't want to send that message the way it is. Sleep on it, son. Come in tomorrow morning. I'll be here. We'll work it out in decent language. All right, son?"

"All right." I took back my telegram and made an effort to pocket it. He helped me. I watched him tear up my message blank.

"You can't say 'fucked up.' It's against the law, huh?"

He nodded. "You don't want to say it, son. You're just tired."

"Yeah. I'm awful tired. How'd you know I was staying at the Y?"

191

"All the soldiers stay at the Y. They're in here all the time."

"Sending telegrams to the Pentagon?" I asked, fighting my weariness.

"No. You're the first. Most of them others just ask their folks for money to keep going. They can't seem to go home. That war over there does something to them. But you know about that."

"Yeah. I know about that."

"You come back tomorrow morning, son. We'll send them a proper telegram, okay?"

"Yes, father." I smiled tiredly at him and with great relief he smiled back at me.

I left him and stumbled back to my room and collapsed in my clothes on the bed. I slept soundly.

○

In the morning I awoke refreshed and hungry. I ate a large breakfast at a nearby coffee shop and then went around to the Western Union office. The old man wasn't there. I was disappointed. In his place was a young, gum-chewing woman. I printed out my message and gave it to her. She read it through once and then a second time, counting the words. This is what she read:

SECRETARY OF DEFENSE
THE PENTAGON
WASHINGTON, D.C.

ASTOUNDED AT THIS UNEXPECTED RECOGNITION OF MY COMBAT SERVICE. AS REQUESTED I WILL ATTEND THE WHITE HOUSE CEREMONY ALONE. I HAVE NO FAMILY. MY PRESENT ADDRESS ON LEAVE IS THE SLOANE YMCA 34TH STREET NEW YORK CITY. THANK YOU.

SINCERELY,
PVT. DAVID GLASS
U.S. ARMY

"You were in Vietnam, huh?" she said.

"Yeah."

"Rough, huh?"

"Yeah."

"A straight telegram will cost you six seventy-five. A night letter two-fifty."

"Send it straight." I handed her a ten-dollar bill and she gave me the change.

She sat down at the teletype machine and began to clack out my reply. I watched her for a moment and then I interrupted her: "Where's the old guy who was here last night?"

"He's on nights. Comes in at four."

"Would you do me a favor?"

"Sure. If I can."

"When he comes in show him my message. Would you? He'll understand."

"Sure thing."

I left her typing out my message and went out into the warm summer morning. I felt let down and relieved.

○

How can I explain my acceptance of the White House honor? It turned out to be quite simple. Before I sent the telegram that morning I had mulled over several inflammatory replies, though none as outrageous as the one induced by grass that the old teletypist had refused to send.

(1) Your records are in error. I did not destroy an enemy machine-gun unit and kill four of the enemy. Perhaps this recognition belongs to another Private David Glass in your files and I cannot accept his citation. (I did not believe there was another Private David Glass in the United States Army in Vietnam.)

(2) Please review the recommendation for this high honor. I do not recall my involvement in the incident you cite. (Ridiculous.)

(3) I am not a hero of your war. I do not believe in your war. I cannot . . . (The FBI would be on my ass in ten seconds.)

Again I reread the Pentagon telegram and my anger subsided. For finally it was the very absurdity of it that attracted me, excited me; that and the opportunity it offered to meet the President. After all, he was the one man most responsible for that year of my life. I saw myself as a vessel of the inevitable and inevitably I went to the White House.

○

The arrangements by the Pentagon were organized efficiently. On the morning of August 28, a military plane flew me to Washington. A protocol officer met me on my arrival and I was whisked by limousine to the White House. We arrived at nine forty-five, fifteen minutes before the scheduled ceremony in the Rose Garden, weather permitting. The hot weather permitted. It was not equal to the intense heat of Vietnam, but in my dress uniform, buttoned to the throat, I sweated profusely. At the portico of the White House, a cluster of newsmen, photographers and television cameras greeted us. I blinked at the popping flash bulbs as the protocol officer amiably waved away the questions put to me.

"Gentlemen, you'll get time for pictures and interviews at the ceremony in the Rose Garden," he said, smiling. "Just be patient. You'll get the hero with the President." He checked his wrist watch. "In precisely twelve minutes. You'd better get set up in the Rose Garden. We're on a tight schedule."

They scurried away and I was escorted quickly through the corridors of the White House and out into the Rose Garden, where several other young men in uniform stood about chatting with members of their families. They welcomed me with nervous smiles—my fellow recipients of the Medal of Honor. I wondered if they were also selected in error. I noticed one young woman standing off to the side, weeping quietly. The widow of a hero, I decided. Perhaps the widow of a Private Hammer or a Corporal Doll, summoned to collect the award of her heroic husband who didn't return with his bounty of Vietnamese trophies—ears and fingers and toes—to mount on the wall of his TV den.

"This is the head of a VC I killed in the Mekong Delta." Did anyone bring back a head?

We all stood about in that lovely rose garden with the sunlight shimmering through the foliage, creating shadows, caressing the summer roses, as the television cameras were set up to record the arrival of the President of the United States. The GI's and their families chatted gaily; the widow brushed away her tears and comforted her young, bewildered children; I stood alone, finally abandoned by my busy protocol officer, and observed the scene. Into it came the starched and pressed figure of the President. He smiled affably, first at the press corps and then at us heroes and our families. The smile vanished when he noticed the distraught widow. The television cameras were focused on her. The President nodded solemnly at her, trying to exude empathy across the expanse of lawn that separated them.

I suppressed a wild inclination to laugh, and in that moment I knew why I was there. I was going to tell him the truth—the whole truth—in front of all those television cameras.

○

With the President's appearance, the ceremony got under way. Standing behind an array of microphones, he made a brief speech on the general heroism of "our magnificent young American guardians of liberty" and then paid specific tribute "to the young men gathered here this morning, who chose to risk their lives against overwhelming enemy forces."

Pausing, he looked up from his prepared text and gazed down the row of heroes—four soldiers, then the widow and me. "I say *chose* to risk their lives," he continued, his somber eyes fixed on us, "because these men responded to an inner call to duty that no government or people could ask of them. I thank God they survived their ordeal."

His declaration was punctuated by a gasp from the young widow, who quickly pressed a handkerchief against her mouth. Instantly, the cameras swung away from the

195

President and focused on her. His face flushed, the President tried to amend his error only to compound it: "One award today is made posthumously. The brave hero who died serving his country is represented by his brave widow." It brought another painful cry from the widow, and a fleeting scowl of anger creased the President's face as his eyes darted toward the cameras. They were still fixed on the sobbing woman. I could see the frustration stiffen the President's body.

Composing himself, he returned to his text and abruptly concluded his statement. "Today, a grateful nation recognizes its defenders with the highest military award it can bestow—the Medal of Honor." He turned quickly away from the microphones and stood before the first recipient. Two military aides sprang to his side with medals and scrolls ready for presentation. In unison, the cameras turned to catch the action. After each scroll was read, the President selected the ribboned medal from its open case and hung it over the bowed head of the hero, shook his hand, made a quiet comment and moved on down the line. When the procession reached the widow, she listened stoically as the citation was read and maintained her composure when the President handed her the medal in its case.

I heard him say in a low voice. "I'm deeply sorry to have upset you. It was thoughtless of me. Forgive me."

"Thank you, sir," she whispered.

"Please accept your country's gratitude. We are most proud of your husband's supreme sacrifice and share your great loss."

"Thank you, sir."

"I noticed that your children are here with you. Would you come by my office with them after the ceremony? I'd like very much to meet them and have a chat with you."

"Oh, yes sir. Thank you, Mr. President."

Now he was standing directly in front of me, smiling, relieved, as one military aide read the ridiculous citation of my bravery and the other stood by with the medal.

I was the last of the day's heroes. That suited my purpose. It gave me the opportunity to talk to the President at the end of the ceremony. I waited patiently while he placed the medal around my neck, gave me his fixed smile, and said, "Congratulations, Private Glass," and extended his hand. I didn't clasp it.

I kept my voice low so only he and the military aide could hear me: "I'm not one of your heroes, Mr. President. I think your war is an obscenity."

The smile died on the President's face. His hand dropped to his side and his head darted nervously to his right toward three men in dark suits, blue shirts and black ties, uniformed civilians, standing casually several yards from us. I hadn't noticed them before. Instantly, I knew they were his Secret Service guards. At that slight indication of concern from their President, all three men stiffened and tucked their hands inside their jackets. I knew they were fingering pistols. Their reflex action shocked me. I felt the blood rising to my head. My legs quivered. My God, I was unarmed. They knew I was unarmed. What could I do to harm their President? Words were my only weapon. Seeing the alarm in my face, the President jerked his head slightly but emphatically in a "no" sign. The men in blue shirts, their legs apart, stood rigid like coiled springs. I could feel their tension. Yet, around us, no one else seemed aware of it. A few feet from me, the widow was waving at her children standing amidst the group of family members gathered near the television cameras that were busily recording the event. The correspondents, with microphones and pads, awaited the moment to get their interviews. Their attention was on the widow. She was their bet for the day's news story.

As the whole absurd scene cluttered my mind, the President's subdued, sympathetic voice intruded: "You're upset, son. I know what you've been through. I know the horror of war. I know how painful it is for you. But you did what you had to do for your own good and for the good of your country."

Christ, I thought, he doesn't have a clue. As his words sounded in my head, I looked past him at the Secret Service men, stolid sentinels, oblivious to the activity around them, their attention fixed only on their President and me. Their dreadful gaze challenged me. I could not let them deny me my moment. I heard my voice sounding flat, cold, as if it were detached from me: "Yes, Mr. President, I acted for the good of my country. I killed for the good of my country. But I could never have done the things for which you summoned me here. I came because I wanted to talk to you—to tell you the truth about your war."

The President bristled. "Control yourself, son," he said sharply. "Don't be foolish. This is not the place to discuss what's troubling you." His tone softened. "I'll be glad to talk with you later. I'm most interested in what you have to say—but later."

"No sir," I blurted. "Now. Right now! Did you know that General Gunn personally killed three Vietnamese women who were farming their rice fields?"

Surprise flickered on his face and then his eyes narrowed and his thin lips stretched into a hard line. "General Gunn was a brilliant leader—the best. He gave his life for this country."

"General Gunn was a butcher!" I lowered my voice. "General Gunn got a hard-on killing gooks."

The remark struck him like an unexpected blow. His face went white. I saw genuine fear in his eyes as he glanced at his military aide, who responded by gripping the pistol in his holster.

It was that simple, senseless action of the military aide that ignited the scene and led to my undoing.

Recoiling in panic, the President retreated from me, crossing his arms over his chest. In the same moment, the military aide drew his pistol and pointed it at me. My reaction was instinctive. I grasped the muzzle, twisting it down sharply and wrenched the pistol from his grip.

After that, I cannot sift the exact sequence of events. It all seemed to happen at once. I remember the Secret Service men, pistols drawn, moving toward me and hearing the shouts and screams of many voices and then the sharp, popping sound of a gunshot—a sound so familiar to me. A hot, sharp pain from the bullet erupted in my belly. I saw the President, eyes staring—I'll never forget the look of panic on his face—drop down to his knees on that green lawn and press his head into his chest to protect himself. He was a pathetic figure, curled into himself like a fetus. Then the military aide filled my vision, coming at me, and my right hand kicked into my chest as I fired the pistol. I don't remember hearing any more gunshots, only wild screaming and seeing people falling flat on the ground all about me. I must have dropped the pistol because I recall my empty hands clutching my belly. And then someone's fist cracked hard into my mouth and I went down on my knees. A voice shrieked, "You crazy sonofabitch!" and many hands gripped me and pinned me down and pummeled me. I felt the grass pressing against my face and then I must have blacked out.

When I returned to consciousness, sirens were screaming in my head. I was strapped on a stretcher, swaying through the streets. Colored lights flickered. A hot ball burned in my belly and expanded into my chest. The pain made me alert. I looked into the face of a black, sweating, white-coated medic. For a moment, I thought I was back in Vietnam in a med-evac chopper but the white coat dispelled that. I felt the medic's fingers stuffing gauze packs into my gut. I clenched my mouth against the pain. "What happened?" I gasped finally.

His eyes moved up from my belly to my face. He blinked in surprise. "You tried to kill the President, man."

"But I didn't."

"No. But you shot his military aide."

"Bad?"

"Not as bad as you. Just a shoulder wound. He's ambulatory."

I closed my eyes, the pain washed like endless waves over me. His fingers pressed harder into my belly. I grimaced. "How bad am I?"

"You got a big hole in your gut, man. But you're conscious. That's good. If I can stem the bleeding and we get to the hospital in time, you just might make it."

I groaned under the pressure of his hands. It felt like his

199

fingers were calculating the bones in my spine. Away off I heard him say, "You poor bastard." Then the sirens faded in my head and I blacked out again.

○

In the hospital, they saved my life so it could be put on trial for attempting to assassinate the President of the United States.

○

Well, now you know why I'm sitting in this prison cell awaiting trial. Isn't it absurd? And it all happened because I simply wanted to tell the President the truth.

Sure I fired at the aide, but I had to, in self-defense. I was ambushed, with a bullet in my belly, and he was coming at me. I winged him in the shoulder to *deter* him. That's all. I don't have to tell you how accurate I am with a gun.

But you know what they said—*everybody* in that Rose Garden? They said I threatened the President's life. Why else did he retreat from me? Why else did the aide draw his pistol on me? Why else did I wrest the gun from him and fire it as he threw himself between me and the President?

But I ask *you*: why would I want to kill the President in the Rose Garden of the White House in front of all those witnesses? That would be the act of a madman, wouldn't it?

11.

The small, rotund man, half-glasses caught on the tip of his nose, entered my cell and sat down stiffly on the hard-backed chair brought in by the guard and placed opposite my cot. His feet didn't reach the floor. It made him look comical. I pushed the typewriter table aside and sat back comfortably on my cot with my back against the cell wall. He looked at me over his glasses. "I'm Dr. Wily," he said and he no longer looked comical.

"How do you spell that?"

"W-I-L-Y."

"Without the E?"

"Yes."

"Are you as sly as your name?"

He didn't smile.

"You're the psychiatrist appointed by the court to examine me."

"That's right."

"To find out if I'm sane or insane."

"I simply want to ask you some questions."

"Shoot." I grinned.

"What is your name?"

201

"David Glass—like in a pane of glass but I'm not easy to see through."

It didn't amuse him.

He took a small pad and gold pencil from his breast pocket and made a note.

"What did you write?" I asked.

He answered without hesitation. "Patient appears alert and is humorous."

"Thank you. But I'm not a patient, doc. I'm a prisoner."

"Force of habit," he said. "You are a prisoner. Do you know why you are here?"

"There's nothing wily about that question. I'm accused of trying to kill the President and I'm perfectly sane."

"When did you threaten the President's life?"

"I *met* the President in August."

"Do you remember the date?"

"Is this a memory test?"

"It's just a simple question of fact."

"August twenty-eighth."

"At what time?"

"Shortly after ten o'clock in the morning."

"Where did this meeting occur?"

I was annoyed by the simplicity of his questions but I went along with him. "In the Rose Garden of the White House," I said, and added, "I was there to receive the Medal of Honor."

"What is today's date?"

"October sixteenth."

"And where are you?"

I looked puzzled.

"What is this place?"

"The maximum security cellblock of the Lorton Penitentiary in Maryland." I lost my cool. "I don't have to tell the enemy anything but my name, rank and serial number—David Glass, private, United States Army. Serial number seven-six-five-four-three-two-one. Easy to remember and so is everything else that's happened to me in the army." I smiled again. He didn't.

"Do you regard me as the enemy?"

"Let's say I don't consider you a friend."

He didn't pursue it. "You said you're a recipient of the Medal of Honor."

"Yes sir. But I can't show you the medal. It was on a ribbon and they took it away with my shoelaces and belt. They don't allow me to have anything I might use to strangle myself." I laughed.

"What amuses you?"

I pointed at the typewriter. "They let me have that after I came in here. It hasn't occurred to them that there's a long ribbon in that typewriter. Long enough to make a hangman's noose if that was my intention. I only want it to write with. I hope you won't tell the authorities or they'll take it away."

"You have my word. What are you writing?"

"Just some things for my lawyers," I lied. "To help my defense at the trial."

"And when is your trial?"

He was back on the track of time. Did the man know his place in time?

"It's scheduled to start on November twenty-third."

"That's only a month away."

"Five weeks," I said, correcting him. But then nobody was questioning *his* sanity.

He had continued to make notes throughout our conversation but I was no longer curious about them.

"Why did you try to kill the President?"

"I didn't."

"You shot his aide when he was shielding the President."

"That's what the papers say."

"There are witnesses who will testify to that."

"That's their story."

"What's yours?"

"I can't tell you."

"You cannot or will not?"

"I will not."

"Why?"

203

"Because you won't understand."

"Why don't you try. Perhaps I will understand."

"You are appointed by the court to determine my sanity. The court wants me to be declared sane so it can try me and convict me. I don't want to waste your time. I'm sane and I didn't try to kill the President. And I am ready to stand trial."

"Did you serve in Vietnam?"

"Yes. It's where I earned the Medal of Honor."

"What were your duties?"

"I was a combat soldier."

"Did you kill anyone?"

"Yes."

"Who?"

"The enemy."

"How did you feel about killing?"

"It sickened me."

"Always?"

"Always."

"Even on the occasion for which you received the Medal of Honor?"

"Yes."

"Why did you do it?"

"It was my job."

"Was it your job to kill the President?"

Ah wily Dr. Wily. "But I didn't kill the President."

"But you tried to—didn't you?"

"You sound like the prosecutor, doc."

"I put it badly," he admitted. "I am only interested in the state of your mind at the time and not to judge your guilt or innocence. That's for the court to decide."

"I'm sorry, doc. A soldier doesn't give ammunition to the enemy."

"Then you do regard me as the enemy?"

"You're appointed by the court. I consider the court my enemy."

"But I can only express my expert opinion, not fact."

"It comes to the same thing."

"I won't argue the point."

"Thank you."

"Is there anything you would like to tell me?"

"No. But I'd like to ask you something."

"What is that?"

"What is your opinion regarding my sanity?"

"I cannot answer that."

I grinned at him. "You cannot or will not?"

He rested his gold pencil and pad on his lap and smiled the briefest of smiles since the interview began and then shook his head. He plopped forward out of the chair and stood up to go. I remained on my cot, watching him. He paused at the cell door as the guard opened it. "Perhaps, when I return again, you can tell me why you wanted to shoot the President. It might be of help to you and I would like to understand."

I shook my head but said nothing.

He left and the guard locked the cell door behind him.

○

An hour after Dr. Wily departed, my guard informed me that my typewriter would be removed from my cell that night and every night at lights out—ten p.m.—and returned to me in the morning. When I asked him why, he said that was his orders from the warden. Shortly before lights out, I secretly removed the spools of ribbon from the machine and hid them under the mattress of my cot. When the guard wheeled the typewriter outside my cell he was satisfied with his task—and I was satisfied with mine. I slept more comfortably with that small lump of ribbon under my mattress.

○

Dr. Wily visited me once more before my trial. I said nothing about the typewriter ribbon to him. At that second meeting, we went over much the same ground but with greater hostility on my part. The results were the same and I didn't see him again until he testified at the trial. In the interim, I was interviewed by the psychiatrist selected by

205

my lawyers to aid in my defense. They hoped he would learn something more than I had told them. He did. But it had no effect on the course of events.

○

Dr. Goodman was a different cup of tea from Dr. Wily. He was much younger—no more than thirty-five—and less detached, less formal in his approach. In fact, after five minutes, he seemed genuinely concerned about me. In his preliminary questions, he asked me about my health. Did I feel well? Did I sleep well? Was the prison food all right? Was my imprisonment depressing? Did the guards treat me decently? At first his sympathetic approach made me wary, but after a while I responded to his warmth and found myself eager to talk to him. When he began to question me about my childhood—no one had ever done that before—I answered freely.

"How old were you when your parents were killed in the plane crash?"

"Eleven."

"You were a grown boy. It must have been a terrible shock."

"Yes."

"How old was your father?"

"He was thirty-five. I only found out much later in the orphanage. I thought he was a lot older."

"Perhaps it was because you were so young. Parents always seem much older to their children."

I shook my head. "No. I don't think that was it." I stared at him. "How old are you?"

"I'm thirty-five."

"My father looked older than you. I remember his face. It was much more lined and his eyes were older. More tired. You know what I mean?"

Dr. Goodman nodded. "You said he had been in a concentration camp when he was a teenager?"

"Yes."

"I'm sure that nightmare experience aged him."

206

"Yeah. I guess so. Thirty-five's pretty young for a psychiatrist, isn't it?"

He smiled. "It's old enough."

"Yeah. I'm only twenty, nearly, but I feel a lot older."

"You've been through a lot yourself."

"How would you know?" I said warily.

"Well," he shrugged, "you lost your parents. You spent seven years on your own in an orphanage and then a year in Vietnam. That must have been difficult. And now you're here."

"Yeah, and now I'm here."

"Would you like to tell me about it?"

Did they work from a standard set of questions?

"What do you want to know?"

"Whatever you want to tell me."

And a standard set of answers?

"What about the time in the orphanage?"

"The years in the orphanage were okay. I don't think about them anymore. Too much has happened to me since then. It seems like a lifetime ago."

"What do you think about?"

"The year in Vietnam."

"What was it like?"

"Bad."

"What was bad?"

"The killing."

"The killing you did?"

"What do you know about that?"

He met my gaze openly. "I know you got a Medal of Honor for it."

"What else?"

"Is there something else?"

Was he sympathetic or wilier than Dr. Wily?

"Nothing else."

"How did you feel when you killed those four Vietnamese?"

I regarded him curiously and it puzzled him.

"Why did you call them Vietnamese?" I asked.

207

"Weren't they Vietnamese?"

"They were VC, gooks, slopeheads."

He understood. "Is that how *you* regarded them?"

I shook my head but said nothing.

"They were human beings."

"Yes."

"And you didn't want to kill them?"

He was way off the track but he was on the course. Could I trust him? I met his warm gaze. I wanted to confess. "Will you understand?"

For the first time in the interview his eyes took in the manuscript on the floor and then returned to me. "Try me," he said.

"I didn't kill any Vietnamese—no civilians, no Vietcong, no NVA—in the whole year I was there."

He remained composed. "But you got the Medal of Honor for destroying a machine gun and four enemy soldiers. I read the citation."

"That was a fuckup. A crazy mistake. If it happened, somebody else did it and I've got his medal."

That shook him. "You mean you didn't do what they said you did?"

"That's right."

"But that hasn't come out in the papers," he said. Disbelief was written across his face.

"No one's bothered to check it out," I said. "They had no reason to, did they? They believe I tried to kill the President and that's the only killing they're now interested in."

Poor, pathetic Dr. Goodman. He persisted in being rational and persevered with his questions.

"You went to the White House to receive a medal you had not earned?"

"Yes."

"Why?"

"Fate." I hunched my shoulders. "I wanted to tell the President what his fucking war had done to me and guys like me. How could I resist the opportunity?"

208

"And what exactly did you tell the President?"

"What I had done in Vietnam." It was an easy lie.

"And what was that?"

Dr. Goodman regarded me earnestly and in his disturbed face I saw the distraught, furrowed face of my father when he had told me about his years in the concentration camp—experiences I had not understood—and I confessed all. I told him about my first patrol. How Sergeant Stone had cut the throat of that boy and then got killed and decapitated. I told him about Corporal Doll slicing off the sniper's finger and driving us through that ravine like a madman and then getting fragged in the head by cool Corporal Thomas. I told him about Lieutenant Caldron hounding me and about Hammer shooting his captive and trying to kill me. And how I killed Hammer and the lieutenant and Wade and Hawley. I told him about the slaughterhouse and Big Man and General Gunn and Colonel Clay. It gushed out of me and when I was finished I felt the relief that comes only when one has awakened from a terrible nightmare.

Poor Dr. Goodman. My feverish confession shocked him out of his skull. He couldn't cope with it as I hadn't been able to cope with the terrible confession of my father. All he could do was pursue the logic to its absurd end.

"But why did you try to kill the President?" he asked.

"I didn't. I fired at the aide to protect myself."

Dr. Goodman looked more unnerved.

"Do your lawyers know what you've told me?" he persisted.

"No. Only you know."

"Are you telling me that you're on trial for what you didn't do and not for what you did?"

I said nothing to that. We stared solemnly at each other.

He was trembling as he stood up stiffly from the straight-backed chair. He shook his head in sad bewilderment. I no longer saw the tragic face of my father in his. I didn't have to ask him his decision about my sanity. I knew it. Poor Dr. Goodman.

209

12.

My trial lasted three days.

My lawyers, over my protest, entered a plea of not guilty on the ground that I was irrational and could not distinguish right from wrong at the moment of the crime.

Two Secret Service men and the military aide, his arm in a sling, testified that I was aiming at the President when the aide sprang to block me and was wounded.

Television film was presented in evidence showing the moment I fired the pistol.

The prosecution was prepared to call a great number of additional witnesses to corroborate the testimony of the Secret Service men and the military aide but the defense waived the need for further eyewitness evidence to save the time of the court.

Dr. Wily testified that in his judgment I was sane and able to distinguish right from wrong at the time of the shooting. Under cross-examination he admitted that he did not know why I had tried to kill the President.

Dr. Goodman, the only witness for the defense, testified that I was insane and did not know right from wrong at the time of the criminal act. Under cross-examination he said he believed he understood why I had wanted to kill the President but he could not support his judgment with fact. Throughout his testimony, I watched him nervously clasp and unclasp his hands. Poor Dr. Goodman.

My lawyers opposed my taking the witness stand. I did not protest.

No one subpoenaed the President to testify.

In his charge, the judge declared that the conflicting testimony of the psychiatrists was based on opinion, not fact, and he ordered the jury to disregard it in considering its verdict.

After an hour's deliberation, the jury found the defendant "guilty of attempting to assassinate the President of the United States."

My lawyers quickly asked for mercy for me, citing my year of combat in Vietnam and my award of the Medal of Honor for valor "in defending the people and principles of this nation."

I am now awaiting the sentence of the court.

At first, I worried about what the sentence would be. I don't anymore.

Does it really matter?

New York
September 1971—October 1972

About
the Author

Len Giovannitti is the author of
The Prisoners of Combine D, a novel about
World War II which received the American
Library Association's Liberty and Justice Award
in Imaginative Literature, and the co-author of
a political history entitled *The Decision
to Drop the Bomb*. He has lived his entire
life in New York, where he has
worked as a producer-writer
of television documentaries.